Unwelcome Visitors

Slocum's steady hand drew his .44 from the sheath of leather beside the bedroll. Wilma lay on her stomach, still breathing hard. Her face blanched as she looked at him with an unspoken question. Lying on his belly behind the willows with the hammer cocked on his .44, he could not see the two men who, obviously from the sounds, were searching for their camp.

"They can't be far."

"His horse is hobbled. I see it out there with the others."

"Where are they?"

Silently, Wilma frowned at him as Slocum held out his free hand for her to be still. He wanted to surprise the hell out of them.

"I thought you said this getting him would be easy—"

"Shut up."

They must have missed Slocum and Wilma. After shaking his head at her offer of his pants, Slocum eased his way through the willows. He could see the pair standing in front of the tent, their backs to him.

"Hands in the air or die," Slocum shouted.

"What the hell—" The older one cocked his hammer, but when he jerked around, Slocum shot him in the chest and he spilled over on his back. His loaded gun went off in the air. The second man raised the muzzle of his pistol—obviously shaken by the surprise attack of a naked man.

D0802859

DON'T MISS THESE
ALL-ACTION WESTERN SERIES
FROM THE BERKLEY PUBLISHING GROUP

THE GUNSMITH by J. R. Roberts
Clint Adams was a legend among lawmen, outlaws, and ladies.
They called him . . . the Gunsmith.

LONGARM by Tabor Evans
The popular long-running series about Deputy U.S. Marshal
Custis Long—his life, his loves, his fight for justice.

SLOCUM by Jake Logan
Today's longest-running action Western. John Slocum rides a
deadly trail of hot blood and cold steel.

BUSHWHACKERS by B. J. Lanagan
An action-packed series by the creators of Longarm! The rousing
adventures of the most brutal gang of cutthroats ever assembled—
Quantrill's Raiders.

DIAMONDBACK by Guy Brewer
Dex Yancey is Diamondback, a Southern gentleman turned con
man when his brother cheats him out of the family fortune. Ladies
love him. Gamblers hate him. But nobody pulls one over on
Dex . . .

WILDGUN by Jack Hanson
The blazing adventures of mountain man Will Barlow—from
the creators of Longarm!

TEXAS TRACKER by Tom Calhoun
J.T. Law: the most relentless—and dangerous—manhunter in
all Texas. Where sheriffs and posses fail, he's the best man to
bring in the most vicious outlaws—for a price.

JAKE LOGAN

SLOCUM
AND THE TRAIL
TO YELLOWSTONE

WITHDRAWN FROM
RAPIDES PARISH LIBRARY

MN
WPA

J

JOVE BOOKS, NEW YORK

THE BERKLEY PUBLISHING GROUP
Published by the Penguin Group
Penguin Group (USA) Inc.
375 Hudson Street, New York, New York 10014, USA

Penguin Group (Canada), 90 Eglinton Avenue East, Suite 700, Toronto, Ontario M4P 2Y3, Canada
(a division of Pearson Penguin Canada Inc.)
Penguin Books Ltd., 80 Strand, London WC2R 0RL, England
Penguin Group Ireland, 25 St. Stephen's Green, Dublin 2, Ireland (a division of Penguin Books Ltd.)
Penguin Group (Australia), 250 Camberwell Road, Camberwell, Victoria 3124, Australia
(a division of Pearson Australia Group Pty. Ltd.)
Penguin Books India Pvt. Ltd., 11 Community Centre, Panchsheel Park, New Delhi—110 017, India
Penguin Group (NZ), 67 Apollo Drive, Rosedale, Auckland 0632, New Zealand
(a division of Pearson New Zealand Ltd.)
Penguin Books (South Africa) (Pty.) Ltd., 24 Sturdee Avenue, Rosebank, Johannesburg 2196,
South Africa

Penguin Books Ltd., Registered Offices: 80 Strand, London WC2R 0RL, England

This is a work of fiction. Names, characters, places, and incidents either are the product of the author's imagination or are used fictitiously, and any resemblance to actual persons, living or dead, business establishments, events, or locales is entirely coincidental.

SLOCUM AND THE TRAIL TO YELLOWSTONE

A Jove Book / published by arrangement with the author

PRINTING HISTORY
Jove edition / January 2012

Copyright © 2012 by Penguin Group (USA) Inc.
Cover illustration by Sergio Giovine.

All rights reserved.
No part of this book may be reproduced, scanned, or distributed in any printed or electronic form without permission. Please do not participate in or encourage piracy of copyrighted materials in violation of the author's rights. Purchase only authorized editions.
For information, address: The Berkley Publishing Group,
a division of Penguin Group (USA) Inc.,
375 Hudson Street, New York, New York 10014.

ISBN: 978-0-515-15029-2

JOVE®
Jove Books are published by The Berkley Publishing Group,
a division of Penguin Group (USA) Inc.,
375 Hudson Street, New York, New York 10014.
JOVE® is a registered trademark of Penguin Group (USA) Inc.
The "J" design is a trademark of Penguin Group (USA) Inc.

PRINTED IN THE UNITED STATES OF AMERICA

10 9 8 7 6 5 4 3 2 1

If you purchased this book without a cover, you should be aware that this book is stolen property. It was reported as "unsold and destroyed" to the publisher, and neither the author nor the publisher has received any payment for this "stripped book."

1

Slocum's heart beating under his breastbone while he caught his breath sounded like a large Indian tom-tom. Changing hands with his Colt Army model .44, he swallowed, then dried his sweaty right palm on the side of his britches. The sharp traces of spent gunpowder filled his nose. His shoulder pressed hard against the wall of the saddle maker's building; his ears turned to hear the sounds in the night, and he listened hard. A dog barked out on the street—somewhere some men were shouting, "Where in the hell did he go?"

I'm in the alley, stupid. His horse was half a block away, hitched beside the Valley Tribune Newspaper building. By being careful, he hoped to slip down the alley and get to his mount. They didn't know the animal, nor, in all likelihood, had they seen Slocum ride in on him a few hours earlier.

On his move from the saddle maker's building to the rear of the mercantile, he crossed the dark back dock, smelling the sweet molasses feed and feed grain's thick aroma. His eyes adjusted to the starlight even under the porch roof as he slipped across to the far side with some ease. Then the sounds of someone's footsteps moving between the store and the next building came to his ear. In response, he moved to the wall between some crates to conceal himself, his .44 cocked and ready.

"You see him?" someone asked his companion, out of breath and standing in the starlight not six feet away from the porch.

"Hell, no, I wouldn't know him if I saw him."

"Who in the hell is he?"

"Slocum's his name is all I know."

"What did he do?"

"Shot someone over a card game in Gertmeir's Saloon."

"Probably some tinhorn who deserved it. I'd bet he's long gone."

"Let's get out of here. He'd probably shoot us if we did jump him in this damn dark alley."

"Yeah." They hurried back toward the street.

Slocum listened to them shout when they were out front. "He ain't back there."

He moved off the porch. In a short while, he made his way like an Apache through the alley until he was looking at the silhouette of his horse standing hipshot under the cotton-wood branches. Inching his way close to the whitewashed pine siding, he stepped out, undid the reins wrapped on the worn-smooth rail, and put them over the horse's head.

"Easy," he said to the animal out of habit. The gelding snorted in reply. Slocum about laughed. That horse didn't understand anything except that they would soon be moving. His foot in the stirrup, he threw his leg over and, seated, turned the animal north. The bay gelding set into a jog and drew a few dog barks after him. The skin on Slocum's shoulders felt taut as his horse clopped past some dark homes, and he half expected a bullet or a shout to challenge him at any moment. Soon they traveled between the small, fenced, irrigated fields, and a milk cow's bawling broke the night crickets' orchestra sounds.

He smiled, looked back, and saw no pursuit. Satisfied there was no one coming after him at the moment, he sent the bay off in a long lope. The horizon began pinking in the

east over a towering range as it moved closer to sunup. When
he came off the mountain and knew he had only a short distance to go before he reached Marla's place, the tight tension
in his back muscles eased.

The corrals and Marla's low-sided log house blazed in the
first bright light of the sun as he reined up. Marla came to the
doorway in a dress unbuttoned down the front. The dim light
in the shadows showed flashes of her flesh as she appraised
him from inside the house. As she swept her hair back, one
of her pointed breasts became exposed, and so did the half-
dollar-sized nipple on the right.

"Didn't expect you to come home this soon," she said in a
dry, smoky voice. Then she hunched her shoulders and gripped
the dress closed about midway down. He could still see her
cleavage. He dropped from the saddle and held on to the
saddle horn until his sea legs were firm under him. Then he
stepped out and she came over to kiss him.

Finished kissing, he held her and rocked her against him.
"I wasn't coming back this soon."

"What happened?"

"That Townsend kid drew a gun on me in a card game."

"Oh, no." She squeezed him harder and pressed her firm
boobs into him. "His father has all kinds of power. What
now?"

"I better get on my horse and ride. I can't beat him in a
prejudiced court of law."

Her green eyes narrowed and she looked upset at his
words. "But if he drew a gun on you, how can it be a crime
to shoot him?"

"Money and power, like you said, would get me rail-
roaded."

"What now?"

He smiled at her, then with his hands, he gently moved
the dress apart to expose her shapely body for him to look at.
With a mischievous grin, her green eyes sparkling, she stepped
back inside the open doorway and undid the buttons on her
dress. Then she gave a shimmy, and the dress fell to her feet.

She swept the garment up and turned to show him her shapely rump. "Come on, big man, the bed is this way."

In no time, he shed his clothing and boots. The morning temperature chilled his bare skin, and he stepped over to the bed to get under the patchwork quilts. She hid beneath them, holding the covers up to her chin.

He slipped under the bedcovers and soon began to feel her smooth skin and firm flesh under his hands as he slid against her. He sought her left nipple and rolled his tongue around the stiffening point. She rose off the bed for his attention, her mouth formed an O, and she inhaled. "Gawd, Slocum. That's wild."

He moved over her leg and nested between them, his rising erection bumping into her. Quick as a cat, she gripped his prod to push it down and then inside her wet gates. She raised her butt to accept him, and he plunged deep inside her.

"What will I do—" Her words were cut off by his strength, which sent her flying away in a thunderstorm of lovemaking, fired by his regrets—today he must part with this passionate female who was rubbing her smooth belly against his corded one. He drove into her with even more fierce effort than usual, and she responded by crying out to encourage him. Lost in each other, they soared higher than a bank of thunderheads and fought through the updrafts to ride the tops of the sky. Then, at last, he came inside of her and she strained to join him. Like colorful hardwood leaves in the fall, they glided back and forth from one side, then the other, until they landed on earth like a feather.

"Oh," she cried. "I'll miss you, hombre. There are men in this world, but few with your strength and passion. Dear God, what will I do without you?"

"Hire a couple of hands to do the ranch work and find you a new man to share this bed."

"Where?"

"Marla, you weren't looking for a man when you found me."

She swept the hair back from her face and settled on the

pillow. "I was about over the loss of my husband, Rail. You caught me during a rare lapse in the effectiveness of my shield against men moving in on me."

"Any good man could break down your barriers." He laughed, pulling on his pants. "We better have breakfast and I'll ride on."

"If I don't feed you, will you stay longer?"

"No, I need to move on. Mark Townsend will send the toughest men he can hire looking for me when he gets the word that his worthless son is dead."

She shook her head, angrily putting on her dress. "Everyone knows that boy of his wasn't worth a damn."

"Blood's thicker than water. Worthless or not, the old man'll want revenge, and he can afford to hire it."

She raised her chin, busy buttoning up the front of her dress. Working to squeeze her boobs under the material, she shook her head in disgust at her disobeying body. "I know you like them, but at times they get in my way."

They both laughed.

Slocum started the fire in her iron stove, feeding the small strips of wood he'd chopped earlier for her. He'd damn sure miss her cooking, the seasoning and care that went into every meal. Marla was a dream of a person to have shared his life with during the past six months while he helped her work her cattle, cut out and ship the culls, and make the ranch's operation top-notch for her. To have to leave her after all this time and all their efforts tugged on his mind. But there was no other way; he must ride on.

Coffee making was soon completed. He took a steaming cup and went to the front door to look at the mountains for any sign of someone coming for him. Too soon for any pursuit to get out here. With his mouth pursed, he blew on the drink's surface to cool it. "Marla, have you ever been to Cheyenne?"

"Not in years."

"There's a guy named Gary Crane who runs a saddle harness repair shop on Dray Street. Gary Crane, Dray Street,

Cheyenne. Gary might know where I am if you ever need me real badly. I mean real badly. Send him a note or go down there. However, it might be slow, me getting word and then getting back here, but I'd come."

"Send a note to Gary Crane on Dray Street, Cheyenne, or have him forward my letter. Tell him to get hold of John Howard?"

He agreed with a head bob.

Tablespoon in her hand, she looked up at the underside of the cedar shingles on the roof for help. "I hope I can remember all that—if I really need you. All right, I have some huckleberry syrup for these flapjacks." She was soon on her hands and knees behind the curtain on the lower wooden crate cabinets securing the quart of fruit preserves. Out of breath, she rose up holding the blue treasure. "There. The butter is on the table. Don't tell a soul you know about my syrup. I save it for special days like Christmas, and this damn sure is special, to have you leaving me."

His first bite of the pancake and her sweet syrup made him nod. "I see why. That is heavenly. I haven't had any of that since I was a boy in the South. The berries grew on mountainsides, with chiggers, ticks, and copperheads living in the low bushes."

"Rattlesnakes in them up here. It ain't easy to pick enough to make that much syrup."

He blew her a kiss and went on eating. When he finished, she stood up to hug him. "I have some elk jerky in a poke. Also some cornmeal with brown sugar that the Mexican folks boil in their coffee cups for nourishment. Just be careful is all I ask."

With her hugging his waist, they went outside and then she recalled his food sack and went back in for it. When she returned, he secured it in his saddlebags and then kissed her.

Hard for him to release her, but there was no choice. He had to ride off, hide his trail, and get farther away from his enemies. He scratched the too-long hair behind his ear. Marla had planned to cut it when he got back from town. A haircut would have to wait until later. For now, he climbed onto his horse and, with one last salute to Marla, rode away from possible pursuit.

In Buffalo, Wyoming, two days later, he swapped horses at a livery and rode east like he was going to Deadwood and the Black Hills. But he soon circled back south and headed into the Bighorns. He hoped his pony's tracks were lost to anyone who was after him. If they knew his bay horse, he knew the red chestnut he rode now would not fit the description; besides, the livery man was pretty closemouthed. Later that day, he had climbed well into the Bighorns and felt that that would lose most any trackers, save some real Indian ones. He avoided people on his way and made no stops at any small crossroads stores.

He had enough supplies from Marla to do him for several days. The second night in the Bighorns, he camped in the high country off any trail, back in the timber. He expected no one to come around, but the sound of horses on the move in the night awoke him. He quickly put on his boots under the stars and went to his own mount. He didn't need the animal to start nickering to the others. Keeping him quiet might prove hard since the sorrel had not seen any others in two days.

But he kept his hand on the horse's nostrils and whispered to distract him. The half dozen riders with high crown hats silhouetted against the night sky filed north in a line with four packhorses behind in a hard trot. Moving at night, they were more than likely an outlaw gang heading out to rob a mail train or make a big heist of some bank with lots of money in its vaults.

From Browns Park down in western Colorado to the north end of the Bighorns along this trail, lots of outlaws hid out. Most of them were Mormon boys in their late teens who were shunned into exile by elders who didn't want them taking the eligible wives from the supply the pluralists drew from. These young exiles had a hard time finding any work in this tough country and turned to joining the outlaw gangs. The first place the law went to look for them after a big robbery was in the whorehouse district of places like Denver. Since they weren't going to be future customers anyway, the houses bled them of all their money with rollicking sex, high-priced liquor, and fine, expensive meals. When all of their dough was gone, they were turned over to the law with busted heads and shrunken balls. They would stumble out the front door of some grand Victorian three-story mansion into the arms of the local lawmen, who promptly called in the U.S. marshals, and then the local police collected the hefty rewards on their arrests.

Simply business in the West. Horny young men flush with their ill-gotten riches went to the whorehouses, had a helluva a good time, and when that loot was gone—they robbed again. Usually they were led by clever men who had escaped the claws of legal authorities for long periods of time. Such men stayed in hiding or snuck off to places where they were unknown, like Chicago, for a taste of all the flesh and parties their money could buy. The underlings, meanwhile, were incarcerated in state pens like the one near Laramie, the Deer Park freezer in Montana, and Colorado's finest steel bars and cement. Wyoming Territorial might have been the easiest to escape. Lots of men went out through an unlocked door there with the paid-for assistance of an insider and were whisked away by relatives on waiting fresh horses. Few of them were ever returned, and no record of their recapture showed on the prison books.

The band of thieves had passed by him in the starlit night. Satisfied at last that they'd gone on north, Slocum returned to his cold blankets and slept till dawn. He felt satisfied that the gang was not coming back that night anyway.

Next day, he took the road south. They called it the Owl Hoot Trail or the Outlaw Underground Railroad that went through Wyoming, Utah, and Arizona. Wanted men used it to slip off into Mexico. That afternoon he stopped at the first small outfit he came to. A woman in a brown dress was using a shovel to divert irrigation water into the rows of her well-kept garden.

"Hello, stranger," she said, busy with her garden-watering operation and the shovel. "Can I help you?"

"Could you sell me a meal?" He dropped out of the saddle, knowing these were pay-as-you-go-operations. No doubt she was a sister-wife in the LDS Church. Her blond hair was straight and shoulder length, and her pale face needed a little powder and some lip rouge. That all cost money, and her husband likely wouldn't bring her any such frivolous items. Since the man probably only saw her every three to four months, she didn't need it. Slocum could see the muscles in her slender forearms. They were hard muscles; he'd bet there would be no fat on her body underneath the wash-worn brown dress either.

"My name is Jennifer Duncan."

"Nice to meet you. I'm Slocum. I can change the water when it gets to the end of the row if you want to go prepare the food."

She agreed and handed him the shovel. "When you see the water's going to make it to the end, change it. I don't have lots of water to waste."

"I can do that, Jennifer."

She swept her hair back behind her ears. "Slocum, huh?"

"That's my handle."

"I'll remember it. Not many folks drop in here."

"I take it that's right. I ain't seen a soul in days."

"Mister, if they're looking for you, they won't ever find you up here."

"Whatever," he said, as if that was unimportant.

She shuffled to the house in her clodhopper shoes that peeked out from under her hem, which she held up out of the dirt as she walked. Those shoes looked so stiff he knew they had to be pinching her feet. He went to changing furrows. No need to mess up and waste her water.

She was gone for quite a while, then he saw her go up the hill to the source of water and put in a headgate to shut off the flow.

"Are you about through?" she called out to him.

He could see she'd timed it right; the final furrow was nearly completely soaked. "This should water the last row."

"Good, I've got something ready for us to eat. Bring your horse. We can put him up and then eat."

"Sounds good."

He led Red over to the corral and unsaddled him. There was hay in the manger and water in a stone trough. Jennifer came over without a word and waited for Slocum with her arms folded.

"You have a horse?" he asked her.

"She's out on the range. I only use her for plowing or hauling in the hay I cut for winter."

"You put all that hay up by hand?" he asked, amazed at the amount he saw stacked around.

She smiled. "Oh, some boys stayed over who were passing through and helped me put some of it up. There isn't much else to do up here."

Wetting his lower cracked lip, he nodded. "No children of your own?"

"No. I never carried a full-term child." She shrugged, walking beside him. "So I am in charge of my husband's Wyoming ranch. My sisters can raise the kids and do those things over in Utah."

"How many wives does your husband have?"

"I have four sisters."

He knew that meant her husband had five wives, including her. This dim trail over the Bighorns must have several travelers going both ways. Folks with faces that fit wanted posters.

He found Jennifer's small house plain, with a lean-to bedroom on the side with bunks. She obviously slept in the living room on the bed covered with a colorful patch quilt, and she did her cooking in the fireplace. There was a table with six chairs for busier times. He could smell the wood smoke that hung in the air from her preparing the meal.

"It is always good to share a meal with a person passing through—better than eating by yourself," she said and showed Slocum where to wash up. He hung his hat on a wall peg and thanked her.

"You almost caught me wearing overalls," she said as he lathered his hands and then washed his face.

"That would not be a big crime," he said, busy drying his hands and face on her flour-sack towel.

"Oh, that would be very unladylike of me."

"Lots of farmwives wear britches—women who have to work in the crops and fields or ride horses." He was thinking about Marla; when she worked cattle she wore overalls and thought nothing of it.

Jennifer raised her chin and then shook her head. "Not for a woman in public places."

"Your home becomes a public place when someone arrives here?"

"Yes."

"Well, what's for supper?" A big smile on his face, Slocum decided there was no use arguing with her about proper dress; he'd never win.

"Roasted ear corn from the garden, green beans, and the last of my salt pork. Oh, and sourdough rolls from the Dutch oven."

"I smelled them. Excellent."

"Glad you're pleased. Let us say grace to the Lord."

"Sure," he said, bowing his head.

"Most heavenly father," she began, thanking him for many things including her guest, whom she referred to as "company"—and finished with, "Amen."

She raised her head and asked, "Are you married, Slocum?"

"No, ma'am."

"Do you have a home?" She passed him the green beans. "Sorry, I ran out of butter last week."

"No problem. No, I don't have a place to live except wherever I am."

"You don't speak like an uneducated man." She rose and went over to the pail to dip a cup of water out, and then apologized. "I forgot, you probably miss your coffee."

"No problem." He knew the LDS did not partake of coffee. "Yes, I attended school."

"I can write my name and read the Book of Moroni, which for a woman is not bad."

"Someone is coming," Slocum said and set down his cob of roasted sweet corn.

She agreed with a grim face. "Eat. I will see who it is."

His curiosity aroused, he followed her to the door, wiping his face on a cloth that served as a napkin. Out of habit, he shifted his .44 in its holster as she opened door and stood back.

Two bearded men with floppy hats sat atop jaded horses in the yard. They were dressed in ragged clothing, and one wore a wolf skin cape over his shoulders. "Hello, Mrs. Duncan. Seed you got company, huh?"

"Yes, I do, Mr. Deushay."

"We won't keep ya. Just wanted to drop by and see if you needed anything."

"No, I'm fine. Don't need a thing."

"He staying long?" Deushay's partner asked, then spit tobacco off to the side of his fidgeting horse. His lower lip and the beard around his mouth were stained with the black traces of the tobacco. Then he hiccupped and nodded.

"I expect he'll stay for a while, Mr. Roberson."

"Well, don't do nothing I wouldn't do." Deushay said. "See you, darling."

His sidekick laughed like Deushay had said something funny, like he knew something Slocum and Jennifer didn't, and the two men galloped away. Jennifer collapsed against the door frame.

"Who are those two galoots?" Slocum asked.

"Two crazy, filthy old men who live up here in the mountains. They come by every so often when they're drunk and

scare the life out of me. Talking nasty and spitting tobacco."
She shivered, and Slocum caught her.

He looked down into her face. "Have they ever hurt you?"

"No, but I don't trust them. I sleep inside even in the summertime and bar my doors when I am here alone."

He looked hard at her. "You ever tell your husband that they scared you?"

"Yes. He said when they come at me to shoot them. I can't hardly shoot a coyote, let alone a person. He doesn't know how bad they are. He's never seen them."

"Still, you better keep the gun handy. Those two are half—or more—raw animals."

She nodded with her face pressed against his vest, and he felt some of the tight-muscled tension slip away from her.

"I'm sorry I bothered you with them." She drew back and then guided him back to their meal. "Eat before your food gets cold."

She only picked at the food on her plate and shoved the remaining food in the china bowls at him. "Let there be no waste."

No doubt the two men had struck fear in her heart. Slocum decided that he'd let Red rest a few days and do some work around the place to help her out—and to see if they came back. "When is your man due here?"

"Two, three months. He'll bring me supplies in October before the snows begin, and take the cattle back with him. Then I'll be locked in here until spring."

"Ever get lonesome?"

"I have a Bible and the Book of Moroni to read. I try to stay busy. I make quilts and clothing. I'll shoot a deer and hang it. An elk is too big. I pray a lot too."

"You know you haven't eaten enough?"

"Enough for me. I'm fine. I am grateful you were here though."

"No problem. How many cattle does your husband have up here?"

"Maybe sixty head. It's just summer range. They do good

all summer on the rich grass, but I have no way to feed hay to that many. I keep my mare up in the lot and shed her during the bad weather. We share the winter."

"A few years ago I spent a winter up here, farther north." He had no intention of telling her it was with a Cheyenne woman. "Wind sure howls."

"You know the ways of these mountains, then. I'm grateful for every warm day."

When dark came, she showed him to a bunk and said she hoped he slept well. In the distance, a timber wolf howled somewhere on the mountain, and Slocum decided that ought to make her fidget as bad as her earlier grubby company. His boots and socks off, he wiggled his toes. Maybe he'd get more than a few hours' sleep during the night. His gun belt hung handy to him on the upper bunk post and, finally down to his one-piece underwear, he crawled into the bed and under the covers. It would be cold by daylight in this high elevation, summer or no summer.

He awoke. Not sure why at first, but then he felt the presence of another person in the room. Starlight shone in through a small four-paned window, letting in enough light for him to see Jennifer's form in the doorway.

"You can't sleep?" he asked.

"No."

"Come get into the bed. We can keep each other awake."

"No."

"I won't bite you. Company is better than being alone."

"Not right."

"I guess we only answer to each other." He propped his head up on his elbow. He thought she must be wearing some long cotton gown.

"And to God."

"I understand, but if you aren't going to sleep, come and I'll hold you. You can get up anytime your conscience bites you."

She laughed. "It is biting me now for talking to you about it."

"Oh, the shame of it. Two grown people talking about right and wrong in the dark when no one else knows anything about it."

"He does. God does."

"What are you going to do?"

"If you promise me you won't force yourself on me—I'll share your bed."

"Good enough. I swear—"

"To who?"

He shook his head when she sat on the edge. "Whoever you want me to."

When at last she lay down beside him, he could feel her shaking and smelled the faint aroma of a woman. "You cold?"

"Cold and scared."

He curled around her and in minutes he fell back asleep. A few hours later he awoke and could again smell the faint scent of woman. He held her securely in his arms on the narrow bed, and he wondered if she realized the danger lurking between them: his rock-hard erection.

Taking a deep breath, he rolled over and gave her his back. He decided that she wasn't ready for anything more than sleeping yet. *Be patient*, he told himself. He slept some more with her form pressed against his back. That was damn distracting, but he did manage a little more sleep. No need for him to be in a rush.

He half woke when she moved hard against him and threw her arm over his shoulder. A sound from outside made him start and listen. Was someone out there?

She started too and whispered, "You hear something?"

"Stay in bed," he said softly and slipped out from under the covers. His bare feet were silent on the rough board floor, and his fingers closed on the grips of his .44. The Colt slipped soundlessly out of the leather sheath, and the hammer made a slight sound when Slocum cocked it back.

Someone was coughing not far from the front door when he slipped across the room, dark save for the starlight coming in through the window. He heard some deep breathing, hard soles scrambling on the ground, and then something hard struck the door. Those idiots were trying to ram down her front door.

"Get the hell out of here!" Slocum shouted when they rammed it again.

"That him?" The question sounded gasped out between their hard breathing.

"Hell, yes. Get to the horses."

"Ow. You dropped it on my foot." The victim went on moaning.

"Get to running."

The bar over the door proved jammed despite Slocum's efforts to remove it while holding his gun, so he set down the revolver and strained to push the bar up. He heard the drum of horses' hooves galloping away and swore under his breath. The holding board finally gave way and the door swung open. He grabbed the revolver and shot into the night's darkness, swearing at the intruders' retreat.

Jennifer came to the door, wrapped in a blanket, and touched his arm. "Was it them?"

"Deushay and Roberson? Yes, I think so. They got away. I couldn't get the door open fast enough." From the doorway, Slocum could see that the heavy post they'd been using to batter the door was lying on the ground where it must have fallen on one of the intruder's feet. No doubt it had hurt—the ram was no small stick.

"They ever do this before?" he asked, herding her back inside.

"They never tried this." She lit a candle and set it on the table. "Have those two lost their minds?"

"No telling what old hermits like that are thinking."

She let the blanket slip away and hugged him. "What can I do?"

"Load your pistol, if you must remain here."

"I can't leave." She hugged him tighter. He felt her thin body against his. The hard mounds of her small breasts under the flannel gown pressed into him. In a trembling voice, she asked, "Oh, my God, what will I do?"

He released her and rebarred the door. Satisfied that the security was in place, he turned and pulled her up into his arms. As he passed by it, he blew out the candle. "They won't be back tonight."

"Where are you taking me?" she asked in a small girl's voice.

"Where do you think?"

"Back to bed?"

"Yes."

"Oh." When he set her down beside the bed, she started taking her gown off over her head inside out. "Help me out of this thing."

He did and she began to unbutton his underwear like it was nothing at all. With her hands, she pushed the garment off his shoulders. Bending over, they bumped into each other and laughed as she helped him undress. Then she pulled him into the bed on top of her. Reaching around him, she covered them with blankets against the cold air and then lay back down in the narrow berth. He raised himself up and she moved in place under him.

"I'm glad that attack is over." She squirmed frisky-like underneath him.

He rested in the V between her legs and felt his rising sword grow larger between them. She reached between them to catch his prod, then eased the head of his dick inside her wet gates. "Go easy on me, please."

"Of course," he said, braced over her, his swelling probe slowly entering her. The core of his brain was ready to explode and his heart quickened with each second of progress as he pushed deeper inside of her with each small thrust. The entryway was tight and her efforts to meet him grew more furious until, at last, his swollen dick went past her ring of fire. Oh, she was proving to be exciting. He settled in to enjoy his meeting with her internal parts. Whew! She was tight, and excited for him to pound her ass.

2

Before dawn cracked the sky, Jennifer was up with a candle reflector lamp, making oatmeal and more biscuits in a Dutch oven. Slocum pulled on his pants, then went outside barefoot to vent his bladder. His face washed by the cold air, he hurried back inside. She looked up at him from her cooking in the fireplace and nodded.

"Thanks. I did sleep. I'm grateful."

"Don't mention it. It was very nice."

She blushed in the firelight and shook her head. "I'm sorry. I was upset about their—"

"Good." He went and dressed, buckled on his holster, and rejoined her in the big room. She wore the blue flannel nightdress that he figured she put on over her head and that went down to her ankles. She set a bowl of oatmeal before him, the cereal smelling of vanilla and cinnamon with some brown sugar on it. The enticing aroma as well as her blackberry jam on the biscuits made the saliva flow in his mouth. She silently ate some of the hot cereal from her bowl while he looked at her.

"You mad about last night?" he asked her. "You haven't said much this morning."

She swept her blond hair back behind her ears. "No, I guess being alone out here I don't talk to myself very often. So with you here, I realized how much I keep my mouth shut."

"The food is good. I saw the woodpile yesterday. I'll split some more cooking wood for you."

"That would be generous of you."

Outside after breakfast, he sharpened the two axes with a whetstone, then went to splitting blocks to make smaller sticks to use for cooking. Pine split easily, but it also burned faster than the hardwoods that did not grow in these mountains. He was swinging the axe as a shot rang out.

The bullet struck his shoulder blade like a sledgehammer, slamming him to the ground, and his shoulder felt like it was on fire. Half-conscious, he could hear two men talking—the hermits, Deushay and Roberson. Slocum lay facedown in the dirt, not daring to move a muscle.

"We got him! We got him!"

Sour sawdust in his nose, Slocum didn't move for his .44. His left shoulder blade felt like it was on fire. The two hermits were right there in the saddles on their fidgety horses, stomping all around.

Where was Jennifer? Did she have her pistol?

"We got him. He ain't moving. Is he dead?" Roberson asked, all excited.

"Shut up. Where is that little bitch at? I want her." Then Deushay gave a silly laugh like a screech owl—both of them were drunk and crazy.

"Get off my place. . . ." It was Jennifer's voice. *Oh, no,* thought Slocum right before he dropped off a dark cliff into a pain-filled nightmare.

How long had he been out? Where they still there? Slocum couldn't hear them laughing like crazy loons anymore. His shoulder still felt like it was on fire. How bad was the wound? He had no idea but the blood drying on his back made the skin tight. His whole upper left side was on fire. Where was Jennifer? Had they raped and murdered her? If they had—

damn, it hurt to raise himself up—he'd make them pay for all of this when he found them. He struggled to his feet, light-headed.

The door of the cabin was wide open when he staggered inside. "Jennifer?"

No answer.

He was not ready for what he found. Weak-kneed, he stood looking at her form sprawled on the bed, naked from the waist down. Not moving. Her blue eyes open wide, staring for eternity at the underside of the cedar-shake ceiling. At the sight of her, Slocum closed his eyes to shut out the vision of her before him. Those damn worthless cowards had raped and then killed her. The blue cast to her face told him they must have smothered her.

How could he, one-armed, ever dig a grave for her, let alone lug her out of here? The clock was ticking for him. He needed to put her in the ground. There was no one to help him dig that grave. The slug in his back needed medical attention or someone to treat it. No way could he do much of anything. His stomach curdled inside and he thought he'd puke.

Where could he go and find the help he needed?

He collapsed in a chair. The fire in his back about blinded him. He hugged his left arm. There was no way to escape the pain raging in his body.

At the table, he used a small pencil to scribble a note on the back of an old calendar.

> *Two men named Deushay and Roberson raped and killed Jennifer. I was shot and have gone for help. If anyone finds her, maybe you'll see that justice is served by ending those two men's lives.—John Slocum*

The note written, Slocum went over and covered her up with a blanket. That would have to do for now.

His stomach churned as he staggered out the door and then closed it. He caught himself on a hitch rail to try to clear his blurring mind and jumbled thoughts. It took a great effort for him to get to the pen, and he still had to catch the horse, saddle him, and get up into the saddle.

He pushed for the gate, then his knees buckled and he passed out. He awoke with his face in the powdered horse shit and, too dry-mouthed to spit it out, he wanted to clean it away, but gave up. On his hands and knees, he used the rails in the gate to crawl up to stand.

The next few minutes were all a blur to him. He recalled catching the horse, and perhaps the smell of his blood caused Red to break away with Slocum clinging to him. At last he somehow bridled the animal, feeling the deep, hot flashes in his shoulder, and one-handed tossed the saddle on him.

No easy deal, the girth gave him hell, but when at last it was in place and tight, Slocum grasped the horn, clenched his teeth, and climbed aboard. Bent over the horn, he could hardly control Red to keep him from running. Jerking on the reins sent jolts to his shoulder, but at last he brought the horse down to a jog. Unable to concentrate, he let the horse have his head.

Late in the day he found a valley and rode toward a thin stream of wood smoke coming from a chimney. He tried to see if the smoke was real, but his vision was so blurred—at last he decided it must be real.

Then his blurred vision faded away entirely, and the rest was lost.

He opened his eyes and looked up into a red-faced woman who hovered over him. "Who shot you?"

"Two crazy murderers."

"Who?"

"Deushay and Roberson."

"Them two sonsabitches?" Her brown eyes flew wide. She gave off lots of body odor when she got close; bathing must be a luxury she seldom indulged in.

He nodded. "They killed Jennifer Duncan."

"Oh, my God, no. They kilt her?"

"Raped and killed her."

"Them no-good bastards. We've got to get you inside so I can look at that wound. It's bleeding again."

"I can crawl," he said with some effort.

"No, you can't. Help me get you up."

He struggled with the big-breasted woman until she was under his good arm and half supporting him. They moved as one in a wobbly fashion for the cabin doorway.

"Your man around?" he asked.

"I ain't got one, 'less it be you." She laughed aloud at the notion.

"Oh."

"Here, lie down on the bed. Facedown. I've got to see about that wound. When did they shoot you?"

"Early this morning. I just rode for help. She needs to be buried."

"We'll get to that later. Man, that shirt is plastered and stuck to your back."

"Don't worry about the shirt." He was lying facedown on the quilts, which smelled strongly of her body odors. She worked at peeling his shirt away from the skin. Once she had the shirt cut off him, she crawled off the bed, talking to herself about some whiskey she had cached somewhere.

"Man, you're a big sumbitch," she said when she returned. "This is going to burn, but I want to try to stop any infection."

The cold liquor made him tense, then it set fire to the wound. Moving in and out of consciousness, he jerked when she found the slug embedded in his back muscles, probing with the point of a thin-bladed knife.

"It ain't deep. I can get it out. Can you stand the pain?"

Weak and sweating, he nodded and clenched his teeth. He felt the bed give as she climbed on the mattress to work on him. When she started to dig for the slug, he let out a scream. Then she got off the bed, and the lead bullet fell into the wash pan with a *clunk*. He passed out.

When he awoke it was dark save for a flickering candle on the table and the fire in the fireplace, which threw orange light into the room.

"You're coming around?" she asked.

He could see that she was taking a sponge bath. Her large breasts rode on top of her ample belly. Slocum looking at her naked as she used the washcloth didn't seem to bother her. She might as well have been dressed. But he was grateful that, if she was going to be close to him, she wouldn't smell so bad.

"I guess you were passed out when I disinfected that wound. I poured some gunpowder from a couple of your bullets in that wound and set them on fire. You feel that?"

He nodded. "Thought you blew me up."

"That cauterized the bleeding too. Tough way, but without a doc closer it was the best I could do. I got some chicken soup for you. They say it cures anything. Want me to set you up?"

"I need to piss worse than anything."

"I've got a thunder mug under the bed. Can you stand up there by the bed? I'll help you."

She came over, still dripping, naked as Eve, and bear-hugged him against her large boobs to set him up, then lifted him to stand. He stood on wobbly legs as she undid his britches, then with her index finger drew his soft tool out. She then bent over and set the pot at his feet.

He must have pissed a gallon. The relief to his bladder made him weak-kneed and she helped him sit down. He softly thanked her.

She shrugged on a dress to cover her nudity. "Hell, I thought I was going to need to build an ark before you got through."

He laughed even though it hurt. She went over to the fire-place and dipped out a steaming bowl of her soup. Then, armed with a spoon and the soup, she came back to sit down on the edge of the bed, making the bed ropes squeak under her.

Spoonful by spoonful, she fed him until he was so sleepy he thanked her and quit eating. She rose, went over for her bottle of laudanum, and fed him a spoonful of it.

"You won't care in a little while. You need to rest."

The last thing he could recall were her large, dark, rosette nipples under the thin material close to his face as she bent over him, settling him in the bed. Then he fell into never-never land and slept until morning.

She was cooking breakfast when he managed to sit up. No way to clear out his fogged-up head.

"I'm going over and give Jennifer a burial."

"I—"

"You rest. You ain't fit to do anything. I can't load you on your horse when you're passed out. I've dug enough graves in my life. I sure as hell know how."

"Be a tough job. You know her well?"

"Not well. But we met and talked some. I mind my own business. She minded hers."

He nodded.

"There's oatmeal up here, you want to chance walking over here to the table."

"I'm going outside to piss first."

He regretted that statement. Bracing himself as he reached the door, he wished he'd used her pot. But finally, dizzy and light-headed, he was able to piss off the porch by hugging the post. Then she held his good elbow and guided him inside to the table.

The oatmeal stuck to the roof of his mouth. Her roasted barley coffee hardly moved it for him to swallow. When he'd eaten all he could, she gave him more laudanum, and then, with him back in bed, she rode off to bury Jennifer. No need to protest her doing something he couldn't do in the shape he was in. His eyelids shut, and when he woke in the afternoon, she was still gone. He collapsed on the porch after emptying his bladder, then he crawled back inside over the rough-sawn boards and got on the bed to wait for her return.

Past dark she came in, after having put his horse in the corral. "You still kicking, big man?" she called out as she came into the cabin.

"Yes. You all right?" he asked.

"My back won't be the same, but she's buried." Hands on her hips, she stretched her back muscles.

"Sorry. Did you catch any sight of those two?"

"If I had, I'd've busted some caps at them. Did you know that poor woman was smothered to death under a pillow by them bastards?"

Slocum nodded, so weary he knew he wouldn't last much longer without falling asleep.

"They had her body to rape, why kill her?" she asked, sounding bewildered by it.

"I don't know."

"How is your shoulder?"

She walked over and removed the blanket from his shoulder. With her hand she felt his back for any sign of fever, then smiled. "So far, we're winning the battle."

"Thanks."

"I'll wake you to eat. You need to eat."

He nodded and slumped back down on the bed. His shoulder complained, but he ignored it. Weary of his down condition, he wanted so badly to be well again. He slept until she woke him to eat some brown beans.

During the next few days, his strength slowly returned. He began walking around her rough homestead to recover his depleted strength. A sponge bath came next, and while his shoulder still hurt, he could sustain the discomfort and quit taking the laudanum.

He finally learned her name was Wilma—no last name. She wasn't sure of it since she'd been married several times and never divorced.

"I buried three of them. Neal had been shot, another had a heart attack and a stroke, and the third died due to his own damn foolishness."

"What do I owe you?" he asked, sitting across from her, eating some fresh venison she'd shot with his rifle.

"You leaving?"

"I want to run those two down."

She put down her fork and shook her head at him. "And faint off that red horse and get killed falling in some canyon? You better wait awhile and get your strength back, mister."

"Maybe you're right."

"Damn right, I'm right. Why, a kid could tackle you off your feet."

"You think those two're still in the country?"

"Sure. They probably don't think anyone found you or her except the magpies and some mangy, starving coyote. By the time that lazy old man of hers got up here, she'd be rotted and he'd never know what kilt her. There's no one but you to point a finger at them."

"Is there any law up here?"

"What could they do? Dig her up? You'd be the first and last suspect they had."

"You're a lot of help," he grumbled and went back to using the side of his fork to cut up the venison on his plate.

Shaking her head, she took his plate and cut the meat into bite-sized pieces for him

"Make you feel any better, I'll go along and back you arresting them when you're stronger."

He shook his head as if lost. "I'll get stronger."

No need to think about it until he was more himself. He simply hated to admit she was right. The deer meat didn't taste bad at all. "Where are they at, do you know?"

"I guess over near that Cheyenne battlefield where the army fought that bunch they found after the Little Bighorn catastrophe."

"It's in a long, high meadow west of the divide that goes to Ten Sleep?"

"Yeah. You've been there?"

"I spent a winter with an Indian woman up there. There's a big spring east of that site."

Busy eating, she nodded her head and the stringy, graying hair swished in her face, forcing her to take her hands and gather it at the back of her head. "You've been there."

He nodded.

"Where were you headed this time?"

"Oh, off down into Texas, I guess, before I was snowed in up here."

She nodded and snuffed, "Uh-huh."

"I shot a guy over a card game up in Montana. He was drunk, and he challenged me. I had nothing else to do."

"That's called self-defense." She was waving her spoon at him.

He shook his head. "Not when your father's rich and the most powerful rancher in the country. He didn't take the shooting of his heir very good."

"That's what I call good ol' boy law."

He agreed and finished eating. He wanted to be well, wanted to be on the trail of the killers—but he hardly had the strength of a pup. Damn.

3

His wound was healing and Wilma found a shirt big enough for him to wear. To build up his strength, he chopped cooking wood for a few hours each day. Wilma, with the help of a stout horse, had dragged in lots of dead trees to be cut into firewood. She wasn't going to run out with her huge stockpile of logs and stacked wood. But Slocum wasn't ready to tackle a saw job. The effort would require two hands, and his left side was still sore.

One day two men showed up. One was blond-headed and looked like a real lady-killer. His partner was dark-eyed and didn't miss a thing. Both were in their thirties and dressed in suits.

No names were shared. The blond one seemed very open and talked with a pretty smile. His partner said little.

"What in hell happened to Jennifer Duncan?" the blond asked, showing a big smile.

"Tell them about what they did," Wilma said with toss of her head at Slocum.

"A couple of crazy men, Deushay and Roberson, shot me and then raped her. Then they smothered her with a pillow."

28

"Those lousy bastards," the blond said and looked at his partner with a scowl.

"Ain't they in that shack up on the mountain?" his partner asked.

Blondie nodded with a grim look on his face. "I get them in my rifle sights, they won't have to worry about anything ever again."

"Maybe we need to pay them a visit?" his partner asked him.

Blondie agreed and they each shook Slocum's hand. The blond one hugged Wilma and promised some action. They mounted their thoroughbred horses and galloped off.

"You know them two?" she asked after they rode away.

"Not sure."

"That's the Sundance Kid and Butch Cassidy, who're in the Hole-in-the-Wall Gang."

"I guessed so." He'd had the notion through their whole visit who they were.

"There were some breeds who were really bothering a woman and her daughters who ran a small hotel and café over by Yellowstone. That gal sent word to them two about the breeds bothering them and folks say that in a few weeks, those troublemakers disappeared from the earth." Wilma laughed. "I expect them two to have the same experience."

"If they ain't too busy lining their pockets, they may get to it."

"Aw, hell, them boys are just living off robbing the fucking railroads and banks. Who loves either of them institutions?"

"No one, I guess." He still didn't take any threat by the outlaws toward those two killers as very serious.

Then she stretched her arms over her head. "I know I ain't pretty or neat like some gals, but you get hard up, give me a nod."

"I will," he said.

She sent a coy smile at him. "You'd be surprised as hell at how good I am in bed."

"I don't doubt it."

"I ain't in no rush."

She left him and went inside. He'd noticed she'd done a few things about herself. She'd taken to brushing her graying hair and she even wore a better dress around the cabin and took daily sponge baths. All this time while he'd been trying to get back his strength, he had not really suspected her agenda. The cabin looked more orderly. Dishes were done after every meal. The blankets from the bed were aired out on the line several days a week. They didn't smell so sour.

The next few days, she sawed blocks off several logs and rolled them to Slocum's chopping area for him to bust into firewood. Amazed by her strength, he kept to his firewood project. He resharpened her one-man crosscut saw, and she beamed when the teeth grabbed the first log she cut with it.

"That's twice as easy as before," she said, going back and forth with her long saw. "I'd swear that was a miracle."

He agreed and went back to making kindling. At the sound of horses, he looked up. He hissed to her and rested his hand on his .44. The saw stopped behind him. Three Indian bucks came out of the pines and approached.

"Know them?" he asked over his shoulder.

"No. Never seen them before." She joined him.

"Wonder what they want."

"Damned if I know."

"Ho," the older one said and slid off his paint horse. He landed on his moccasins and held a single-shot rifle in the crook of his arm. "We want buy whiskey."

"I ain't got none," Wilma said. Shaking her head at them, she made a shooing motion with her hands.

"No. We want buy whiskey."

"She don't have any," Slocum said to the brave.

"All white men have whiskey."

"No, we're Mormons," Slocum said to him.

"Mormons," the Indian said in disgust to his partners. The other two shook their heads with frowns.

The leader bounded back onto his horse and jerked his mount's head around, and the Indians galloped away. Slocum shook his head and hugged Wilma's shoulder with his good arm, just about ready to laugh. "First time I ever said that to anyone."

"Quick thinking," she said and kissed him hard. He held her buxom form against his body while their mouths sought each other's. The effects of the kiss began to spark reactions inside him.

Pulling apart at last, they gained their breath, still holding on to each other, and he looked to see if the bucks had kept going. They'd disappeared in the timber. No doubt they were renegades, off of some reservation where they belonged. Relieved that he and Wilma didn't have to fight them, Slocum sighed, and his breathing came easier.

"Let's go into the house," she said. "I'm still trembling inside."

He agreed and picked up the axes, and she carried the crosscut saw on her shoulder. Before they reached her cabin, he looked back to be sure. No sight of them.

She heated water for coffee and he had to agree they'd been lucky. Seated on the ladder-back chair, he felt lots of anxiety as she built a hotter fire under her coffeepot, which was hanging on a hook over the blaze in the fireplace. In a short while, the water boiled and she added real ground coffee. Something she'd hoarded, kept back for special occasions. Digging around in a trunk, she found a bottle and, sweeping the hair back from her face, she laughed.

"I knew I had some lightning."

"I think we both need a shot of that."

"Amen," she said, gathering up her dress and heading for the dry sink. After pouring the liquor into tin cups, she delivered Slocum's to him. They clunked cups and tossed their drinks down.

With a smile written on her fresh-looking face, she looked him in the eye. "I think we've earned a toss in the hay."

"And waste that real coffee?" He grinned at her.

"It won't spoil." She began unbuttoning her dress. Slocum got to his feet and toed off his boots. The inevitable was coming and he aimed to make the best of it. Besides, it had been more than two weeks since his last bed adventure.

Undressed, she tied her hair behind her head with a leather thong and turned the bedcovers back. He stripped off his clothing, then stepped over and slapped her bare butt to herd her into the bed.

She obeyed with a nervous laugh and settled on her back, waiting for him to climb in on top. Under the covers, he rested on top of her belly, and she raised her knees on either side of him.

He kissed her on the mouth. Her eyes flew open as if she was shocked, but she soon clutched his face for more and rocked underneath him. His half-filled shaft found her deep, wet pussy and soon slid in the gates.

She squeezed her eyes shut. Then her mouth fell open in pleasure when he found her ring of fire and passed through it. She flattened her legs wide open and hunched toward his efforts. His fury grew and hers flared in response. There was a lot of woman underneath him, and he wasn't missing any of her as her muscles inside began to contract around his thick tool. Her clit began to scratch the top side of his erection. Her breath came in deep draws, and the result was all a part of their intercourse. Despite his effort to hold his weight off of her with one arm, her large breasts shook under him.

Then he knew his time drew toward the end. A tingling in his balls said he was about to come. He gave her a deep shove, and she clutched him tight enough that his shoulder complained. Then he exploded inside her, and she cried out, "Yes, yes."

She pulled him down and smothered him with kisses.

When they had untangled at last, he sat on the edge of the bed, spent and pleased.

She took two tries to get up and soon was sitting beside him. Her calloused hand squeezed his leg and shook it. "I never thought something that good would ever happen to me. It was better than any of my honeymoons with any of them others."

He reached around and forced her to look at him so he could kiss her. He just about laughed at her wide-eyed look of shock. Good for her.

4

No way could Slocum leave Wilma at home. When he mentioned that he wanted to go check on those two killers' location, she told him she had to go along. They caught her thickset horse and saddled him along with Red. With some deer jerky tucked away for him to gnaw on, Slocum planned to make a quick run up to Deushay and Roberson's place and observe them.

He tied on his bedroll in case the errand ran over into the night. He took his .44/40 rifle that shared his pistol cartridges, loaded it, and slammed it into the scabbard under his right leg. Wilma wore men's waist overalls under her dress. Her part-workhorse jogged beside Red, who trotted. They left Wilma's before daybreak and crossed over the crown of the Bighorn Pass by the time the sun came over the Black Hills far to the east. They traveled through brushland covered in sage, and she led him across the mountains and took a path off to the west.

"That valley far over there is where the army and the Cheyenne fought." She tightened the string that held her felt hat on against the growing wind and pounded her horse with her heels to move on.

"Their place is in this valley ahead and back to the right up a canyon at the base. There's no good way to cross over to get to them, so we'll need to approach it from the mouth of the canyon."

"Sounds good enough."

She smiled. "They could be gone or out roaming around looking for more mischief."

He nodded that he'd heard her. Two worthless tramps had murdered and raped a good woman. As long as they breathed free air, Slocum aimed to dog them down. Besides, since they'd shot him in the back, he owed them enough lead to stop their breathing.

Slocum and Wilma dropped off the slope and took a dim, twisty road down through the pine timber. He kept his hand close to his sidearm and studied the evergreen-covered slopes for any sign of a threat. They emerged on a flat, and she tossed her head to the right.

"They up there?" he asked.

"That's where the small lake and spring are, as well as their cabin."

He dismounted and took the field glasses from his saddle-bags. "I'll go take a look."

With Red's reins safely clutched in Wilma's hand, Slocum started up the canyon on foot. There were some tracks in the dirt of the two ruts, but none looked very fresh. He continued the hike up until he could see the low-walled cabin. He focused his field glasses on the small structure—he saw no smoke, which meant they either were not cooking or were gone. Since there was no sign of any saddle stock, he doubted they were home.

He moved in to examine the area at closer range, staying next to the timber, and made his way toward their camp. After a half hour spent lingering near the cabin, he could not see any activity, nor any stock. He found the back door barred on the outside. He removed the lock, then pushed open the door to a room that stank of green hides and trash. Opened tin cans were piled around and left where they had been emptied. Nothing looked worth a damn in the dimly lighted interior—pigs lived better than this. He went out and reblocked the door.

He caught the sound of water falling, which made him wonder, so he went to see the source. The fall of a sheet of water over a rock rim held back a couple of acres of lake. Shame that such bastards had control of such a neat place. If he rooted them out and Wilma wanted to move here, he'd help her do that. He slid downhill on his boot heels and headed back for her and the horses. Where were the grubby residents?

"They weren't home?" She rode up to hand him the reins to Red.

He shook his head. "Place is a mess. They haven't been there in several days. But it's a nice enough site."

She nodded, looking disappointed at the distant cabin. "It would stink like them two for a long time."

"It could be resettled."

"I'd burn it down." She turned away and shook her head.

So much for thinking she'd like this place for herself. They headed back for her place. They would not get back there before dark.

"We may need to find a campsite and ride on back to your place in the morning."

"You disappointed that they weren't home?"

"Yes. I'd like to settle with them."

She chuckled and shook her head. "You may never see them again."

"Oh, I will. I'll hound them down."

"You may have to."

He turned in the saddle and looked over the open sage-brush. A mule deer was headed for the timber and soon disappeared.

"He'd've been good eating," she said, riding her horse close to him.

"We'll shoot one before we get back to your place."

"That'll be fine. There's a small stream to water our horses

ahead. Plenty of grass for them to eat. We can camp there tonight."

"Good. Lead the way there."

The valley she took them to was lined with fir trees on the
slopes. The water looked like a silver stream when they rode
up the flat valley beside it. A couple of moose threw up their
heads and moved out from where they must have been grazing in some marshy spots. The male looked like a trophy.

"Glad you didn't shoot him," she said, dropping out of the
saddle at the campsite. "That sumbitch would have taken all
summer to make jerky out of."

They both laughed, stripping out of their latigo straps and
unsaddling. He rolled out his bedroll and she gathered some
sticks to build a fire. They gnawed on her jerky and later
drank some tea made from shavings off the bar he located in
his saddlebags. Seated side by side on the ground with their
backs to the log, the reflective heat in their faces as the high
country temperatures dropped, they savored the hot tea.

"I've been with several men in my life. You are the calm-
est one to be around. I've been with the I-don't-care kind,
others who ignored me unless they wanted to rut, a few slave
drivers who needed everything done for them—right now.
But you—you make a note that I'm here and don't demand
much. That's relaxing to me."

Slocum smiled and recrossed his boots out in front of
him. "You don't talk all the time either. I like that."

Then he heard something and hissed at her, "Get out of
the firelight. Now!"

She rolled to the side and scrambled to get behind the log.
His hands closed on the rifle stock and he levered in a cartridge.

"What is it?" she whispered from the dark.

"I'm not certain. But I heard something. Lay low." He
handed her his Colt. "Be ready for anything."

His ears strained to hear over the crickets. Who was out
there? Stars had begun to sparkle. No moon yet. *Who was
out there?*

5

On guard all night, Slocum woke Wilma before dawn.

"Sorry, I had to sleep some," she whispered. "Have you seen them?"

"A little sleep won't hurt us." He squatted down on his heels. "I suspect those three Injuns are out there. I brought the horses in closer."

"What are they waiting on?" She got up on her knees and swung the blanket over her shoulders for warmth from the chill in the air.

"Nerve. They're getting it up to take us on or they'll ride off. They're really all concerned about their medicine. Superstitious as hell. An owl can call and they say, 'Bad time to attack them.'"

"I sure hope this is a bad time. I've been up here for several years and never had any of them give me a minute's trouble."

"So have I. But hell only knows what goes on in their brains. Their way of life has been totally changed from what they were used to, when they were able to follow the buffalo and fight their enemies for land usage. Braves were hunters and warriors, not farmers like the government proposes."

"There are no more buffalo to amount to anything. Or any other game like it was before."

"That's it. They are disposed of and spit upon. Breeds even more 'cause they are the spawn of their own traitorous tribal women lying with the white man. They are neither white nor red and have less of a place in this closing world."

"What the hell do we do about them?"

"I hope they ride on."

"If they don't?"

He shook his head ruefully. "I won't bury them."

With a nod, she asked, "Is there coffee?" She indicated the pot on the edge of the fire.

"Not much coffee left. It'll be daylight soon, and we'll see what they plan to do."

"Whatever. I ever tell you that you're my favorite guy?" She gave him a big smile in the dim light.

"Don't brag on me. I'll disappoint you."

She looked at the lightening sky and shook her head. "No, you won't—"

From the corner of his eye, he saw the flash of a paint horse—moving away. "I see them. They're headed west."

She rose, hugging the blanket to her. "Where are they going now?"

"I have no damn idea." He removed his hat and scratched his scalp. Single file, the bucks disappeared between the lodgepole pines. "I guess their medicine was bad."

"Sonsabitches," she swore. "They simply went away?"

"I'm not complaining. Let's load up and go back to your place."

"I agree. Damn them to hell anyway."

One more incident—he was glad he didn't have to kill them. Not that he felt they were special or anything. They were simply lost people, like himself, looking for something. They all shared a lonesome world. At least he had a buxom woman who tried her damnedest to please him, while those three had nothing but their hands to jack off with. He kissed

Wilma for being there, and she went around blinking her eyes like she was in shock over his actions.

The two of them saddled and loaded up. In ten minutes they were headed for her place. No sign of the three bucks, and Slocum hoped they were gone forever. But doubt about them, and the two men Slocum was hunting, rode on his mind as they headed southward. *Where in the hell were Jennifer's killers?*

6

Clouds floated overhead all day, harbingers of some storm headed for the Bighorns. The thought of a severe disturbance made Slocum's belly crawl. When they reached her place, it was near dark. But slung over his lap they had a fat doe he'd shot an hour before. They'd need the meat, and Wilma also spoke about riding in to a settlement for coffee beans if he had some spare money.

He laughed and agreed he had enough money to buy coffee and a few other luxury items.

"Take me a day to get down there and another to get back," she said. "I'd ride your good horse and be faster, but someone might notice him."

"Hey, I'll be fine. Nothing's going to eat me."

She made a soft smile. "You can't tell."

"If it's not storming, why don't you go tomorrow?"

"Fine."

They strung the deer up and began to skin it. Taking care, because he didn't like his venison tasting like hair, he used a sharp knife, then slipped his blade under the hide and made his cuts from the inside. She nodded in approval at his style.

41

"That will sure make for less hair on the meat. Never saw it done that way. Who showed you that?"

"A Cheyenne woman."

"You've had some good teachers," she teased.

"Oh, yes, some good ones."

The deer's body was finally free of hide and he gutted it, saving the heart, liver, and kidneys. When they were laid out, he took the carcass up to wash it below Wilma's spring.

"We can hang it under a wet canvas and keep it cool enough not to spoil," she said, walking along beside him carrying the rifle—just in case.

There was plenty of liver to fry, so they used her meat keeper to store the doe on a hook overhead. The log building, she told him, had repelled bears in the past, and he agreed it was well constructed. Door closed and latched, they went to the cabin.

After supper, they kissed and played on her bed. He was getting used to her thicker body and enjoying her more. At last they undressed like starving people at their first meal and tested the bed ropes under the mattress to find some relief from their cravings.

Sprawled on her back in the flickering light of the candle afterward, Wilma gave a sigh. "I waited twenty years for this to happen to me. I'd hitch up with some guy and think, 'This is going to be like heaven.' But until you came, I had always misjudged it."

"What was wrong with 'em?"

She shrugged. "There were some who thought they were pigs and made it go quick. Others who mauled me like I was some sow. Some couldn't get it up and some couldn't get it down. I've been in the hands of losers too long."

He got up on his knees, and hoisted his half-stiff dick up into his right hand. "Ready for more, princess?"

"God, yes."

The next morning she was ready to ride for the nearest store with ten dollars from his cache.

"I'm going to shock the shit out of that old man," she said. "You tell me how a stranded woman like me could ever have earned ten dollars."

"Let him think you boarded some outlaws who passed on through coming from a robbery. He don't need to know more."

Seated on her horse, she slit her eyes against the bright sun. With a smile, she nodded. "That's all he needs to know. Rest up while I'm gone. I'll be needing you badly by the time I get back."

He laughed and waved her off. With the leather string holding her hat on in the gusty south wind, she rode east and down the slope. Wilma was all right.

With her gone, Slocum sawed off wood blocks all morning and busted them up in the afternoon. The sharp one-man saw dug deep in the dead pinewood. Later, the double-bitted axe swung high over his head and sliced the wood into clean-looking pie-shaped pieces. It was good work for his tender shoulder and should build him back up. Stacking all the fire-wood under the roof of the firewood shelter, he had soon had enough of the labor and walked up on the hill above her place to look around.

She'd soon have enough wood, but it was always possible it could be a bad winter and the snow could stay on long. A person had to be sure the wood would last; cutting and busting wood in a blizzard was no fun.

From the high spot where he stopped, he could see the tall, threatening thunderheads coming fast in his direction. The big storms he dreaded were rolling in like a super freight train over the mountains. Could be hail in them, being that high, and maybe even snow. He'd seen snow in mid-August in this land. Never lasted long, but it could even cover the ground.

He unhobbled Red and put him in the corral for the night as a precaution, then went to fry himself some venison for supper along with some new potatoes from Wilma's garden. They had had some onions the night before to go with the liver. When she got back, he thought perhaps they should go on a raid over to Jennifer's watered garden. That food would only go to waste anyway.

The meat was sizzling, and the onions browning with the potatoes smelled sweet. A boom of loud thunder pealed across the sky like a cannon shot, and he ducked as if to avoid being hit by it. Then the hail began to fall on the roof like hard beans rattling in a jar.

Someone started pounding on the door and yelling to be let in.

Slocum went and lifted the latch. There were two wet punchers in Texas batwing chaps holding their hands over their hats to keep from losing them to the bouncing thumbnail-sized hail.

Once inside, they drew off their battered hats and nodded at Slocum like water-soaked rats.

"Pull up a chair. I've got some hot water to make tea. Ain't a drop of coffee in the cabin." He put the bar of tea on the table along with his jackknife, then went for cups of hot water.

"My name's Densel Smith and this is Hobby Ward."

"Slocum's mine. Nice to meet ya. But what brings you boys clear up here? Kinda outa the way, ain't it?"

"A mite," Smith agreed. "We're going back to Texas. Wanted to see some new country."

"Lucky you two found Wilma's cabin here. There aren't many up in these parts. Wilma will be back tomorrow."

Smith raised his eyebrows. "You ain't her man?"

"I'm passing through too."

"What's a woman who lives up here without a man look like?" Ward asked.

"Respectable."

"Guess that's good enough. We stayed up north a ways with a Mormon woman for a few days, and she mentioned Jennifer as the woman who lived down here."

"Her place is five miles or so south of here."

Ward shook his head. "Wow, we'd've been mashed by that damn hail before we got to her place."

"She's not home."

"Where did she go?"

"Two men killed her about a month ago." He went on to explain about her death and about the pair of killers.

"You say you went to their place and they weren't home?"

"That's right. But I'll get them."

"What in the hell do they look like?" Smith asked.

"They wear rags. They're bums and worthless. One's got a wolf hide he uses for a cape. They ain't had a bath in two springs and got tobacco all over their beards."

"Yuck. They sound like they'd make me puke," Ward said.

"They ain't worth a spent cartridge," Slocum said over the roar of the storm outside. "I've got some fresh venison hanging in the shed. I can slice some more off and cook it if you two want some more. We can share this meanwhile."

"We didn't come to leech off you folks."

"Ain't no leeching. A man comes to my door, I'll feed him. So would Wilma. Good woman."

"What in hell's she doing up here? She got cattle or something?"

"No, she just ended up here is all I know. She'll be back tomorrow night. Went to get some supplies like coffee and things we ran out of."

"Boy, this would be a tough place to have to winter in," Ward said with a shake of his head.

His partner agreed. "I'd go crazy up here."

"Better rattle your hocks for Texas, then. In six weeks there'll be a chance of snow in these parts."

"Hell, that rain outside is bad enough to spook me. They have tornadoes in these mountains?"

Slocum dished out the food onto three plates. "I reckon they have them all over the West and South."

"Listen to that hail and wind out there. Makes my hair stand on end." Smith threw his hands up when the thunder crashed down. "Whew, it's bad out tonight."

"Just be grateful you aren't out driving cattle in it."

"I am," Ward said. "Mighty nice of you, feeding us and all."

They ate in silence, but the storm's fury never let up. The persistence of the weather made Slocum's belly curdle some as it kept up the onslaught outside. Did Wilma have some shelter wherever she was in this storm? No telling. But she was a survivor, and he hoped she'd found some.

In a while the letup came. The two men went out, unsaddled their horses, and brought their gear inside. Then they put their horses up with Red. Slocum stood under the porch during the process. The rain had slowed down and the thunder moved off in the distance.

"That was one helluva of a rain," Smith said as all three of them went back inside.

"Still lots of hail on the ground."

Slocum agreed, but eyed the men a little. He kept his wondering to himself about why those two were this deep in the mountains if they were headed back for Texas. It didn't add up.

"You got any whiskey?" Ward asked, rubbing his mouth like he needed some.

"No. There were some breeds hanging around up here asking for some the other day."

"Guess this being Mormon country it's pretty dry."

Slocum shrugged. "I guess it may be in short supply on account of that."

"That Peterson woman we stayed with back up north of here. She was out too," Ward said.

"Guess you'll have to wait till you get back to civilization to get a good dose," Slocum said as he took a seat on a kitchen chair with his back to the wall.

They laughed.

"You ever met them outlaws that hide out up here?" Ward asked.

"Who's that?"

"Cassidy and the Sundance Kid."

Slocum shook his head. Did they think they were bounty hunters enough to capture those two, or were they wanting to join them? He'd heard of rewards as high as ten thousand dollars on each one of them offered by Wells Fargo and the railroad express companies. But he sure wasn't getting mixed up with them. It was good way to end up with his boot toes pointed at the sky.

"Train robbing would sure beat punching cows," Smith said.

Slocum nodded. "If you survived 'em."

"Hell, most of them do," Ward said.

"I've done some crazy things in my life, but never got into that business. Too old to start that now." Slocum aimed to settle that matter.

"How far is their place?"

"I'm not sure. Don't know them. Don't aim to know them, and they can do whatever they want."

Ward shook his head. "Guess you never wanted to live better than just being in some old shack like this."

"It's dry, warm enough, and I'm not looking back all the time for a lawman, railroad dick, or bounty hunter on my back trail. Boys, I'm going to bed. Been a long day."

Still unclear about what they really were up to, he slipped the .44 into bed with him, making sure they didn't see it. Until he knew more about them, he'd sleep light and keep his gun ready. They put their bedrolls on the floor and grumbled around about how a hotel bed would feel better. Ward blew out the candle and they went to sleep.

Slocum was up before the sun shone, got dressed, and went out in the pristine predawn to empty his bladder. He planned on making some flapjacks for breakfast. There was some of Wilma's apple butter to put on them. Best he could do for the time being to feed his drop-ins.

Back inside, his guests grumbled around and dressed. The skillet on the stand in the fireplace wasn't the easiest to handle when making pancakes, but kneeling next to it, Slocum made it work. Not as good as Wilma could have done, but she was a pro with it. The meal, along with some hot tea, went well, and Slocum's unexpected guests even bragged on it.

"Guess we'll be heading out," Smith said after breakfast.

Slocum wished them well and wondered when Wilma would get back—probably by evening. It took them a while to saddle up and get loaded.

"How far is the next ranch?" Ward asked, tossing his head toward the south before they left.

"Don't know. Jennifer's place is about five miles south of here, but no one's home there."

They nodded, thanked him, and rode out. He watched them leave, still wondering whether they were hoping to join the Bighorn outlaws or something else. No business of his, but there was something strange about the two he couldn't put his finger on.

Wilma rode in sometime past noon, shaking her head over the big storm. She had three cloth sacks of supplies she'd bought. And she rushed over for a kiss from Slocum. "Boy, was that a terrible storm."

"Bad one. You have shelter?"

"Yes, I stayed in a sheepherder's camp with some lawmen looking for a pair they think shot their own boss and took all his money."

"They give any names?" he asked, helping her pack the purchases.

"Ward and Smith. Why?"

He shook his head in disgust. "They rode out of here this morning."

"I bet that was interesting. What did they say?"

"That they were sightseeing the country, headed home. Said they'd stayed with a Mormon sister north of here for a few days and were headed to Jennifer's. I told them she was dead."

"Them three lawmen said they had maybe twelve thousand in currency they stole off their boss."

"Whew, that's lots of money. They simply killed him?"

She shook her head. "Said no one has found his body, but those two were last seen leading his horse and empty saddle headed south. The horse later showed up at a ranch, but no one's found the body of the man. But he ain't been heard from either. He was some real rich rancher from Texas, and the deputies told me there's Pinkerton men all over Wyoming out looking for them two. There's a large reward on them—dead or alive."

"I wondered about them, but I had no idea that what they'd done was such a big deal."

"I guess you'd let them go anyway."

He nodded. "They had me on edge wondering. I slept last night with my gun."

"You reckon they're gone?"

"Oh, yes. We won't see them again. They asked me about joining up with Sundance and his bunch. I simply acted dumb."

She nodded in approval, busy putting items in her crate-shelf cabinets. "I did real good with your money. It went lots further than I thought it would."

He nodded, looking across the open country south of her cabin. "Good. I wonder where those other two killers went."

"No telling. You want to look some more for them?" She came and held his arm and pressed herself against him.

"I'd like to have an idea where they went. Those two will kill again if they aren't stopped."

She agreed and kissed him on the cheek. "I missed you."

He hugged her against him. "It was sort of empty around here. Those two Texans had me wondering what they were up to or going to do."

"Should I pack for a search trip?"

He shook his head. "We'll ride around the next few days and see if we can find any sign of them near here. They may have cleared out, but I doubt it."

"Good, we've got some catching up to do in bed."

He laughed and took her in his arms. "I think so too."

"Close the door," she said and twisted away to go inside.

He did and she began undressing. Waving him over, she quickly shed her clothes and then helped him with his. "I really liked last time, but it only made me want you more."

They played naked, him on top of her, and soon impatient

with him, she inserted his half-full dick inside of her. She spread her legs wide, clutched him, and gasped at his entry. The sparks began to fly from them. The excitement consumed both of them as they raced into a pleasured high. Then he came and they fell into an abyss, lying side by side. So the day went by like a dancing dust devil going right, then left, until they dropped into slumber and woke before sundown.

"Whew," she said, getting dressed. "I thought sex was wham-bam-thank-you-ma'am. I'm still drunk."

He swept his hair back with his fingers, sitting on the bed's edge. "A lot more than that."

"I'm learning. I'm learning."

"You know I can't stay here forever?"

She stopped and looked serious at him. "Yes, I know, but the memories will sustain me."

"I hope so."

She made some oatmeal cookies, and they ate part of the batch after her venison supper. It was dark by then and they fell into bed and slept deeply.

The next morning, he saddled their horses, and after break-fast they began their search of the nearby area for any sign of Jennifer's killers. Several miles from her place on the western slope, he caught a hint of smoke.

"Fire around here somewhere," he said, twisting in the saddle.

She agreed, standing in the stirrups. "A campfire, huh? Where is it?"

"South, I guess," he said, indicating the country to their left.

He soon spotted a sun-browned wall tent with some smoke swirling on the ground around a cooking fire. A short man with hair graying at the temples stood in the flap with a rifle in his hands. He wore a four-crown hat with a nearly flat brim and had the look of someone tough.

"Hold up. We ain't looking for trouble," Slocum said, riding in his direction. "I'm Slocum and this is Wilma."

He swept off his hat. "Carlton Houston, ma'am."

"We're looking for two grubby men who murdered a woman," Slocum told him.

"Several of them up here."

"Deushay and Roberson."

"They're camp robbers. They recently raided my things. I went after them and shot at them, but my horse hurt his leg in the chase and they got away down in the canyon."

"When was that?" Slocum asked, stepping off Red.

"A day before that storm." He set his rifle aside.

"What did they steal?" Slocum looked around the sage-brush-clad mountaintop site.

"Oh, a good pair of field glasses. Some money I had in a trunk and probably some more of my personal things. Would you like some coffee?" he asked Wilma.

"Sure. How long have you been up here?" Dismounted, she looked around at his setup.

"I came down from Montana about a month ago. Why?"

"Oh, I usually know most of the folks that populate these mountains."

"I haven't met many people. Those two came around and I was suspicious, but I've been searching for a trophy mountain sheep. I was told there were several in the Bighorn Canyon."

"I've seen some around here," she said and took a place on his log seat near the campfire.

"I have sugar and cream."

She shook her head.

"Do you know about hunting mountain sheep?" he asked Slocum.

"I've shot some down in Sonora. They're good eating."

"I imagine they're tasty, but I'm looking for a trophy head to mount."

Slocum nodded and sipped on his coffee. He swallowed, then looked over at the man. "This sure looks like the ideal country to find one."

The majesty of Bighorn Canyon yawned beyond them, a deep gorge in the earth that went down to Ten Sleep—not

Ten Sheep as some called it. Indians named the spot that was ten nights from Yellowstone and ten nights from Fort Laramie. Midway point between the two places. A few ranches, a store, and two saloons were all that was there to mark the place, which sat far down in the large chasm.

"You got any notion where those two killers are at?" Slocum asked the man.

"No, but I'll help you look for them. Those scoundrels."

"We didn't bring any camping stuff with us. But we'll bring some back in two days and take you up on that offer."

Houston smiled and nodded at Wilma.

"Sounds all right to me," she said, rather like she enjoyed the attention of both men.

"Oh, I am certain if we put our wits together, we can round them up."

"You must come from England," she said. "You have a trace of that accent still in your talk."

"Yes, my dear, I came from there, but bless my soul, I got to come to America, and my older brother got the moldy old family castle to keep up."

She slapped her knees. "By damn, you got the best deal all right."

They all laughed.

After the coffee was gone, Slocum and Wilma thanked Houston and started back for her place. Slocum knew it would be past dark before they rode in. Crossing over the mountain on the dim wagon tracks, he could see into the trashy lodgepole forests, and the way looked so jumbled with dead and fallen down trees, one could hardly get through them even on foot.

They spooked a large male moose out of a swampy area, and he snorted, then thought better of it and ran off into the trees. His huge trophy rack was widespread, and how he went anywhere, how he could even go through the woods, amazed Slocum.

"Big bull moose, wasn't he?" Wilma remarked.

"A winter's meat supply."

"He would have been. You ever eat any moose meat?"

"Similar to elk, isn't it?"

"Lot like it. I liked buffalo too, but they're about all gone."

"You ever get to hunt them?" he asked her.

"My first man married me, I figured, to make me his buffalo skinner. And I skinned lots of 'em, but them things were too big for me to turn over. I worked all the daylight hours skinning, then fed fires all night to keep the damn wolves from ruining the hides. And in between all that I satisfied the needs of his dick. He'd get a damn hard-on skinning a damn buff out there on the prairie in the broad daylight. He'd come up behind me, raise my dress up, shove my head down between my knees, and ram his prod in me from behind. I thought that was how married folks did it. Till someone said that wasn't how you were supposed to do it."

"How often would that happen?" Slocum watched a big wolf in the edge of some alder bushes tracking along beyond them. He leaned over and eased the rifle out of the scabbard. With Red set down, he raised the stock to his shoulder. When the big male showed his head and flicked his red tongue out as if anticipating them as a meal—Slocum cut the future years off him with a bullet smashing him in his chest. The wolf flew over onto his back, thrashing his four legs in death's final throes.

Wilma gave a whistle. "That was a big sucker. I'd seen him kinda tracking us for a while and figured when you got that lever action out that you aimed to end his making any more pups." Her laughter carried and echoed back. "He was a big old stud who really got too brave for his own good today. I sure like his pelt. Ice won't freeze on his coat and that would make a warm hood for me."

"Ice won't freeze on his hair, huh?" He slid the long gun back into the scabbard and started to dismount close to the wolf.

"That's right. He'll make the best hood I've ever owned." Her face beamed at the notion of owning one.

All at once, Red snorted and acted upset at the scent of

the wolf. Slocum chuckled at him, holding the reins tight to keep him under control.

"Why did you wait so long to make a fuss?" Slocum asked the horse. Then he grabbed the wolf's hind legs and dragged him over close to Wilma. With her own horse hitched to a tree, she ran over to help him. He used a cord to fill the slits he made with his knife between the lower hind leg bones. After he had one leg tied up, Slocum dragged him under a pine. The cord tossed over a stiff branch, he motioned for Wilma to pull the rope up and tie it while he held the bloody wolf in a bear hug up in the air. She deftly tied the other leg with the cord through the slit in it. The animal was now strung up and swung slightly in the stiff wind sweeping over the mountain.

He handed her a smaller jackknife to use to work on the wolf. The strong scent of the animal filled Slocum's nose as they began to slip the skin off his warm carcass. A coppery smell mixed with a testosterone odor wafted toward them and made both Wilma and Slocum fight not to gag. The pelt was in good shape for this late in the summer. The two of them stripped the prime skin away from the dark pink meat of the carnivore. Slocum's hands were full of fur to hold it aside as he used his sharp blade to quickly separate the hide's white underside from the wolf carcass muscles.

The hide was soon off the animal, and he shook it to get the sticks and debris out of it. Then he carefully rolled it up. Wilma cut the carcass down and saved Slocum's cord. Leaving the wolf's remains and stinking guts for the magpies and ravens, she turned to Slocum in the red fire of sundown.

"There's a creek we can wash up in at the base of this hill. He sure stank."

Slocum nodded and finished tying the pelt on the back of his saddle. Red kept trying to sling his head around at him when he mounted. They set out in the dying sun's glow to descend the steep open grassy slope for the creek.

After washing up in the shallow water, Wilma smiled at

him as they dried their hands on a flour sack. "Now was when Ermal usually got romantic."

"You game?" he asked.

"I'm not as thin as I was then."

"Well, you suggested it."

She laughed and began to shed her suspenders. "Hell, yes."

With her bent over and her hands braced on a large boulder, the sight of the red glow of sundown on her amble bare butt drew a smile from his lips. He dropped his own pants, unbuttoned his underwear, and stuck his dick between her bare legs.

Her hand reached under, caught his swinging stick, and slipped it into her slot. A long "Aww" escaped her mouth as he probed her. This was going to be better than he'd expected. She was tight and her ring of fire was swollen. With his hands on her hips to stabilize her, he drove his shaft up inside and she gasped.

"Oh, that feels wonderful," she said.

He agreed. Maybe he'd have to find this Ermal and thank him. No, she'd said he was dead. With fury, he shoved his throbbing dick into her to feel more and more of the hot, tight hole. Each drive made his head spin until at last he felt the end rising out of his scrotum.

His hands tightened on her bare hips. Then from his throat came a moan, and his cum exploded out the head of his dick. She squeezed down hard on his spent shaft, and he had to catch her from fainting. When she turned around at last, she collapsed against him.

"Oh, oh," she moaned. "That was wonderful."

He agreed and saw the sun sink beyond the horizon. They would be late getting back to her cabin.

7

The next day, they picked out things they'd need to take along camping with Houston. They made two bedrolls so they could, as she put it, act decent around their host. Then she mentioned it would be a shame if they didn't go borrow Jennifer's horse and packsaddle.

Slocum agreed and set out with Red to go get the pony, if he could find her. There was no sign of anyone having been there lately when he found Jennifer's place again. The grave that Wilma had made for her looked settled. Lucky for him the chunky mare she used for chores came in looking for some company with Red about then. In no time, Slocum had the packsaddle and panniers on the animal and was headed back for Wilma's place.

It was midafternoon when he got back and the day had proved warm. They packed the canvas panniers full of things they'd have had to leave behind otherwise. Everything was ready by sundown for the next day's departure, and they drank Wilma's fresh-made coffee and sat together on a log in the sundown's red glow.

She elbowed him in the ribs. "I don't ever recall sitting and talking down the sun with a man in my life. All the men

56

I've known were either swinging at me or cussing me out for something they considered important that I had no hand in."

He chuckled. "You've had a tough life, girl."

"I'll damn sure miss you whenever you light a shuck on me." She dropped her face and leaned forward, shaking her head ruefully. "I ain't been around a man yet that treated me like an equal as well as you do."

"Just think about all the good times." He reached over and rubbed her back between the shoulder blades.

"Don't quit whatever you're doing. Man, does that feel good. Those muscles are tighter than a fiddle string."

He went to work using both hands on her backbone and tight muscles. She moaned in a low voice at his attention. Poor thing must have been mistreated a lot in her lifetime.

"Why are you up here by yourself anyway?" he asked, curious about why she was living like a hermit.

She laughed. "A cowpoke named Shorty Harrel was the cause."

"Sounds interesting. Tell me the rest of the story." His hands busily continued attempting to chase the stiffness out of her back.

"I was cooking for some freighters going from Cheyenne to Buffalo. Shorty was the scout and sort of the wagon boss. Well, we got friendly on the road. I guess on the road with no parlor house handy, he got horny too, huh?"

He agreed to get her to continue.

"Well, the third day out he came around where I was cooking and told me about a mining claim he had in the Big-horns. How when we got up there to Buffalo, we could go up here and work that claim. He thought he had a streak of gold and silver." She shook her head and scowled about it. "Course I thought there might be a chance he wasn't lying about all of it to get in my britches. So I went along and he snuck a few passes in my bedroll on the road."

She wrinkled her nose at the notion and continued. "He damn sure wasn't a real lover. I've seen stray dogs stayed hard longer. But I wanted a vacation from being the head cook and dishwasher for those grubby freighters. You never know, this might have been the lucky mine."

Slocum agreed with a nod, then rose and put a few more pieces of dry wood to flare up the fire as the night gathered. He could only imagine how dusty and dirty human bodies got on the road with so few places to bathe in as there were between Cheyenne and Buffalo.

"So after we got up to Buffalo, he brought me up here. We borrowed a packhorse to bring our supplies up and he took it back. There was no vein of nothing in his digging and I knew I'd been snookered, but he didn't come back and three days passed. Then a deputy brought his belongings and his horse up here for me—he called me Mrs. Harrel.

" 'I'm sorry, ma'am, but he—your husband—he must have been drunk and fell down a flight of stairs. Couple freighters said you were his next of kin, ma'am. So I brought you all of his things we could find.'

" 'Was he in a whorehouse?' I asked that boy wearing the badge." She laughed. "He blushed like he had been caught naked at an old maids' gathering and swallowed his Adam's apple a couple of times. Then he said, 'Yes.'

"Shorty had twelve dollars left in one of his boots. Must have saved that back. I found it later. So I set into staying up here as long as I could. That was two years ago. Ain't done bad. Guess being up here alone I got kinda lazy about bathing. Your coming's been a good influence on me. I rejoined the human race."

"Amazing how you ever made it, girl."

"Naw, before this I was married to men that beat me about every night. I've been raped by worthless bastards where I did not even know their names and who left me for dead after they were through.

"See why I stay up here and did without?"

He nodded and turned her to face him. He kissed her and she fell into his arms. At last he hugged her to his chest. "Let's go to bed."

"Damn right. You know we may not get a chance to reconnect since we'll have separate bedrolls on this search."

Hugging her shoulder, he laughed. "I bet we don't have any problem getting away from Houston for some private time."

"Now you're thinking. I'm plumb spoiled by your attention, you know that?"

"I am too."

They undressed and climbed under the covers naked—in minutes they were coupling and fighting their way to some high reward. His piston was pounding her, and she was on the bottom, struggling to give back all she received for him—with all that she had.

Before dawn, they both woke up, hungover from their repeated acts of lovemaking, ate a cold breakfast, and then rode off in the first light to meet Houston.

They arrived at his camp midmorning, and Houston rose up from his canvas chair looking ready to ride.

"Glad to see you could make it," he said, doffing his hat for Wilma. "My horse is saddled and I am packed. I'll be ready in a few moments."

The stout roan mountain horse he rode was under a Western saddle, and a flop-eared jackass bore his packsaddle, bedroll, and other things. Leading the mule, Houston came back to camp in a lope. Wilma had already put his folding chair inside and fastened the ties on the canvas door of his tent.

"Fine, fine," he said, and they headed out for Ten Sleep on a narrow way cut in the towering mountain's sheer face. Houston led since he'd been over it recently and knew the best way to go better than Slocum.

"You ever been down this way?" Houston turned and asked Wilma.

Grim faced, she shook her head. "And I may not come back on it either."

"Aw, we'll make it," Slocum said over his shoulder.

"You know, I'm not really certain right now."

"You'll be fine," he assured her and laughed. But in the

tight spots he twisted around in the saddle to be certain her horse made the necessary steps to get by them. Up where eagles soared, they wound off the top toward a small silver stream that bisected the gorge. Still a long ways down there, and no rails to catch them on the right side. The rock face rising skyward on the left scuffed his boots in tight places.

They rested on a wide ledge and Slocum dropped his reins, skirting his horse and Jennifer's horse under the diamond hitch. He helped Wilma down, knowing with all the tension of the trip that her legs might not stand when she did climb off her horse. He'd seen others who were scared of heights after they'd had to ride down a cliff face. He held her in his arms as she tried to gain her sea legs.

"How did you know I'd be this bad off?" she whispered, looking pale under her tanned face. Her large breasts were shoved into his chest, and she hugged him tight. "I'm getting better."

At last she kissed his mouth, then pushed on him and stood back on her own boot heels. "I'll be fine."

He smiled and left her beside her horse. "Need help remounting, I'll be back."

"I'm fine."

With his stirrup hung on the horn, Slocum tightened his girth a smidge. Satisfied with his checkup of the saddle, he could smell Houston's pipe smoke wafting back to him. The man had squatted down ahead of his horse and was using a brass telescope.

"I hope those bastards still have my field glasses when we catch them," Houston said after Slocum joined him.

"We can hope anyway. Seen any big sheep?" Slocum asked.

"Several, but it's hard to see with this old scope how big their horns really are."

"Those must have been good glasses."

"They cost several hundred francs in Paris."

Slocum shook his head. Trophy hunters' ambitions cost money, but everyone to his own hobby.

"We should be on the canyon floor in three more hours."

"Good. I'm ready to be on the lower level."

"How is she?" Houston asked Slocum in a lowered voice.

"Shaken, but she's tough."

"I noticed that. Do you think I could hire her when this is over? It would sure be nice to have a woman around the camp to help take care of things. I suppose I can ask her."

Slocum nodded. "Do that."

"I'd hate to be flat turned down." Houston put the pipe back between his teeth and relit his bowl with a scratched wooden match and a few puffs.

After a short rest, they all rose, ready to continue. Slocum went back to load Wilma onto her horse. She winked at him and bounded into the saddle. "I'm not done in."

"Good." He clapped her leg, then edged back to Red. Once in the saddle, he waved that they were ready, and Houston's mule began braying either in protest or simply as an ornery jackass complaining. The train was soon moving.

Keeping to Houston's time schedule, they ate a meal about two P.M. along the gurgling stream. Wilma boiled water for coffee, then served it with some cold biscuits and venison. They were seated on peeled logs around the well-used campsite—obviously a site to rest, and no doubt used by many travelers who took this route. Indian and white men alike had no other route they could go; this funnel forced people to use the narrow passage they had just gone over to cross the mountains.

After the break, they rode beside a gurgling stream to Ten Sleep. The sun was almost down when they came up the dirt street and got a look at the businesses the town boasted: two saloons, two stores, a blacksmith shop, a livery, and a house of ill repute. Houston dismounted in front of the larger store, Farr's General Store, and told them he'd be right out— he needed to order some things, and he'd ask inside about the pair they were hunting.

Slocum agreed and looked around. Were those two killers here?

There were some lights on inside the store. A few women, obviously genteel, came out with cloth shopping bags and avoided looking at Slocum or Wilma. *Must be the society ladies of Ten Sleep,* he mused. Three cowboys rode by. They were laughing, obviously ready for a good time. They tipped their hats politely to Wilma. Farther down, the threesome hitched their horses at the rack and clunked up the stairs, spurs and all, to push in the batwing doors of Dutch's Saloon.

Wilma winked at him and looked over as Houston came outside. He said, "We can ride down that lane ahead and camp at Mr. Farr's place."

Slocum nodded and waited for the man to get in the saddle and lead the way. "Sounds good to me."

He wanted to go back to town later and scout the saloons and learn all he could about Jennifer's killers. If those two were in the area, someone had seen or smelled them. He wanted the chance to find them and hoped they wouldn't learn that Slocum and his group were in town looking for them, which could make them run.

After they unsaddled the animals, he and Houston took the stock to water them at the creek. Wilma busied herself building a fire. Slocum noticed there was a stack of split firewood and a stone fire ring.

"Mr. Farr, who owns the store, keeps this place for his customers. Ranchers who come from some distance camp here overnight with their families while they get goods. He even keeps firewood in supply too."

"Smart man," Slocum said. "You ask him about the pair we're looking for?"

"They were in his store two days ago." Houston scowled. "Tried to sell him my field glasses."

"He buy them?"

Houston shook his head. "He didn't know that they belonged to me and didn't know they had stolen them or he said he would have."

"He have any idea where they went?"

"No, but he thinks they're still in the area."

"Coffee is about ready," Wilma said, looking up from where she squatted beside her fire.

Slocum dropped to his haunches. "Those two were in Houston's friend's store two days ago, trying to sell his field glasses."

"Well, damn, they're stupid, aren't they?"

Houston agreed, the orange firelight reflecting off his smooth face. If the man had been enlisted in an army, he would have been a major or higher rank. Slocum wondered how many hours he'd spent pursuing higher education in the quiet halls of some old English university. No doubt Houston had been carefully trained to hold a lofty place in society. No one's fool, he bore himself proudly in the saddle or even in camp—no letdown.

Wilma poured them coffee in tin cups she had on hand. With her own steaming cup in one hand, she rose and toasted them. "Here's to finding them two killers."

"Amen, my dear." Houston held his cup high.

Slocum joined them in the salute. Good notion, but where were those men at? Somewhere out in the night, crickets creaked. Be a nice place here if he didn't feel such an urgency to round those two up before they weaseled out of his grasp. There were lots of places they could escape to from here. All the options gnawed at him.

After a meal of fried salt pork and potatoes cooked in a skillet, Slocum excused himself and hiked back to the village. On his hip he wore the .44, and he had carefully checked the caps on each nipple of the five loaded cylinders. The distance he covered in the starlight was perhaps a half mile. He passed the red light on the porch of the rambling house of ill repute. There was a loud piano tinkling away, the sound coming out of some open windows to invite any listeners into the den of iniquity. He recalled how, on a slow night in Texas, he had polkaed all night long with a bevy of wild ladies until he was exhausted. Then all three of those delightful doves physically forced him onto a bed and raped him. Oh, what an evening.

Dutch's Saloon hosted the same three cowboys he'd seen earlier, drinking whiskey at the bar. They turned and looked him over when he came inside. Then, as if disinterested, they went back to drinking from their glasses.

"Vat vill it be?" the small, mustached man with sharp features asked.

"A beer."

"Ah, you are new here."

"You don't have beer?"

"Na, I have beer. I just don't know you. My name is Dutch." He extended a thin hand and they shook.

"Slocum is mine."

"You look for vork?"

"No." He lowered his voice. "I'm looking for two killers. One's name is Deushay, the other Roberson."

"Dey are trash, I don't allow dem in here." The man drew a mug of beer at the spout. He set the foam-topped glass before Slocum. "Dey were in town two days ago."

"Where are they hiding?"

"Dere are a few digger Indians down on the creek. Dey may be dere."

"Upstream or down?"

"Downstream. What did dey do?"

"Murdered and raped a woman up in the Bighorns."

"I hope you catch dem."

Slocum slapped a dime on the bar. The man shook his head. "To be rid of dem for good, I give you da beer."

"Much obliged," Slocum said.

Dutch moved down the bar and must have told the three cowboys about Slocum's mission. The big talker in the group nodded at him. "I hope you string them camp robbers up. They stole our grub last spring while we were out rounding up cattle."

Slocum nodded and raised his beer toward them. "I'll add it to the charges I have."

"We ain't seen them or we'd've blistered their asses with our ropes."

Slocum smiled. "I'll find them."

His beer finished, he thanked them all and went out on the porch. In the morning, he'd check the Indian camp out. Two men rode by without glancing aside at him. They both wore suits and cowboy hats, and Slocum wondered about their business. Obviously they had come down through the canyon in order to get here. Something about them made Slocum uneasy.

What was their business in this isolated corner of the world? He needed to keep in mind that there still might be men looking for him on account of that Townsend kid he'd killed during that card game. They'd be tough hired guns. Were these such men? He'd been wandering around a lot since the shooting in Montana, all the time hoping his traipsing had masked his trail. Maybe those two had nothing to do with any of his concerns. He'd better head back to camp. They'd be lucky if they found any tracks those madmen had left for them to follow.

Wilma covered her mouth with a yawn when he came back to camp. "You learn anything?"

"They might be in some Indian camp downstream." He dropped onto the log where she had been seated.

Quickly she joined him. "Do you think they're there?"

He shrugged and then bent over to kiss her. His action brought a smile to her face in the firelight.

"No telling, I'll take a look in the morning."

"Damn." Her forehead pressed to his. "You must be the sweetest guy I ever met."

"Must be." He laughed softly.

"Our bedrolls are over on the opposite side of the camp," she whispered. "Let's go find them. Houston's gone to bed already."

"Sounds wonderful." They stole off with her holding his arm tight against her full breast.

In minutes, they were coupled together under the covers against the cooling air sweeping over them. Each one's hungry need became an aggressive desire to become one. His hard pumping grew in force, the vise inside her tightening with each plunge, and she moaned in pleasure. Then he felt a deep squeeze in his testicles. The rising force blew out of the swollen head of his dick, and she collapsed underneath him.

"Oh, my God," she whispered in his ear. "I must have come. I heard about doing that, but I never—oh, hell, that was neat. Whew."

They slept in each other's arms and woke up before daylight even pinked the horizon. He dressed and went off to relieve his bladder. Cool morning air swept his face. Where were Jennifer's killers?

Then he heard some horses, and Houston's mule brayed.

What in the hell was going on back in their camp? He rushed back and unsheathed his six-gun from its holster. Wilma's voice sounded sleepy in the starlight as she hurried to finish dressing and hissed, "Who in the hell is here?"

"I'm not certain. Keep down." Then he set out through the lodgepoles to try and get behind them.

He heard some other horses stomping away from their hobbled stock.

"Where are they?" an unfamiliar voice asked.

The speaker was farther east from where Slocum weaved through the trees, hoping to get closer to them before they discovered him. His way wasn't easy, but unlike as in most of the forest, the deadwood from fallen trees in the immediate area had already been gathered by campers. Then he saw the outline of a hat. Another figure joined that one.

"Hands in the air," Slocum ordered, his pistol cocked and ready for anything.

"Don't shoot!"

"Put your hands in the air!"

"We are, we are."

Cautiously, Slocum moved toward them, uncertain of who they were—but they gave up quickly.

"I got them covered with a shotgun," Wilma said.

"Gawdamn it, we've got our hands in the air."

"Better not flinch," she said.

Slocum disarmed them, but still couldn't read their faces in the darkness. "March over by the light."

"Hell," the shorter one cussed. "She ain't got no shotgun."

"Good thing she don't," Slocum said. "You'd've been magpie bait." He gave the taller one a shove.

Houston was building up the fire when they reached the ring of light. He gave the parade a scowl. "Who did you get?"

"Two sneaky horse thieves," Slocum said.

"We ain't no damn horse thieves," the tall one protested.

"Then what were you doing messing around our damn camp for?" Slocum demanded.

"We heard there were some Hole-in-the-Wall Gang members out here."

Slocum laughed. "What were you going to do with them?"

"Join them. There ain't no damn work up here."

"Sit down," Slocum said in disgust. What in the hell was there about this band of merry outlaws that made so many men want to join them? Best answer he could find was the amount of money stolen by them. The numbers would intrigue anyone. A hundred thousand taken in a Montana train robbery. Even a small share of that would make a twenty-five-dollars-a-month cowboy feel like a millionaire. Those two Texans who had dropped by Wilma's place wanted to join them. Sounded like they'd already committed a murder-robbery featuring their former boss. If they had committed the crime, then they hadn't even had a chance yet to spend the loot. So why join the gang?

No answer in any of it.

When the two strangers were seated on the ground, Slocum uncocked the .44, spun the cylinder around so his hammer was over an empty chamber, and holstered it.

Wilma was making coffee and preparing food for breakfast. Houston was squatting on the ground, still seeming amazed that the two wanted to join outlaws.

"You two have any experience at this train and bank robbing?" he asked them.

"No."

"You know robbers get killed?"

The tall one shook his head. "You don't understand. There ain't no jobs for us. We been from Montana to Colorado and back riding the chuck line and no one will hire us. No money, they say."

"You ever been inside a prison?" Houston asked them, like he was some kinda judge interrogating convicted felons before his bench.

"We ain't been in jail for long," the short one said.

"Prison is a dark, cold cave you can't escape. Food is bad and, over any revolt, you face punishment. They whip people until they break, stick them in a dark hole for months. Chain you to a wall."

"But they ain't getting caught," the tall one said.

"The hell you say. They caught six of them in Denver last month in a raid on a whorehouse. All of them were boys from Utah, shunned by church people and forced to leave Utah. Out of work, they were enlisted to do the hard part of these crimes, while the gang leaders sat on their horses and watched them."

"You ain't been looking for a job." The short one, staring at his boots, shook his head in defeat.

"We've been told no by so damn many people, you'd never believe it."

"Maybe you ought to try sheepherding," Houston said.

"Naw," the tall one said. "They only hire Messicans to do that."

"Maybe you should become miners," Houston said.

Slocum about laughed at Houston's suggestions of jobs for them to try. Those two wanted to do work on horseback—not unloading freight, or pushing a broom, and being under their boss's constant attention. They'd have to change vocations— things were changing in the West. The whole region was getting civilized. Fewer cross-country cattle drives. Trains were replacing them.

These kinds of cowboys were a dying breed, no doubt.

Wilma made bacon, fried potatoes and onions, biscuits in

a Dutch oven, and plenty of coffee. The would-be outlaws ate like starving dogs, and when they finished, Houston looked at Slocum. "Hang them or send them down the road?"

"Ship them out." Slocum shook his head at the hanging notion.

The short one gave a long exhale of relief. His partner nodded that he'd heard Houston's decision and Slocum's choice.

"What're your names?" Houston asked.

"Mine's Skip Hogan," said the short one, "and he's Lay McCoy."

"I don't want to read how a posse shot you, 'cause I don't think you're gun handy enough to be outlaws anyway. I'm staking you ten dollars to get the hell out of Wyoming."

"Why do that?" McCoy asked, looking hard at Houston.

"'Cause, I can afford to." Houston acted affronted by the tall man's question.

"I didn't aim to make you mad—sir. Thanks."

"Now get on your horses and get out of the territory," Slocum said, weary of the pair.

They rose and Slocum handed them back their uncapped pistols. "Don't waste time. You've got enough money to go somewhere."

They soon rode out, and Wilma laughed, shaking her head over the deal. "Are there lots of unemployed men around?"

Houston nodded. "Too many. Makes for mischief like this gang business."

"And I guess we're camped on the way in and out of the Bighorns," Slocum added. What was the world coming to?

"Where are those two killers?" Houston asked.

"Somewhere around here. I may find out something about them by checking around."

"I need to stay here," Wilma said. "Wash dishes and clean up."

"I'm going back up in the canyon and look for a trophy for the day until you find them," Houston said. "If you don't need me."

Slocum shook his head. "I can look around myself. You find that grand buck."

"Oh, I'd like to before they break off a trophy horn fighting."

So they parted. Wilma to wash dishes, her clothes, hair, and body, and to get the camp set up to suit her better. Houston went ram scouting, and Slocum went off to find out where the killers had gone.

Ten Sleep's farrier and blacksmith, a big man, was beating on a red-hot iron rod. When Slocum entered, the smell of burning coal assaulted his nose. The man halted his work. "What can I do to help you?"

"A little information."

The man stuck the rod back in the red coals of his forge and shed his gloves. "What's that?"

"Two hermits recently killed a woman up in the Bighorns. Their names are Deushay and Roberson. They were headed down here."

The big burly man nodded, turning his handiwork over in the red coals and fire in his forge. His face was blackened by the coal stains and smoke.

"I know them. Weird bastards. They came by here two days ago. They were headed for the badlands west of here. They have a place out there. Somewhere west and south of the main road. I heard they have hot water springs they take baths in."

"No idea where their place is located?"

"I've never been out there, but it's a ways beyond the canyon mouth. If you've never been out there, it is *malpaís* country. Won't grow weeds in a rainy season. Lots of different colored bare rocks."

"You sure their place is south of the main road?"

"They said south—sorry I can't tell you more. Why did they kill her?"

"Raped her and I guess didn't want any witnesses left behind. Smothered her with a pillow."

"Damn, they need to be hung."

Slocum agreed with a nod. But no one was going to do that—but him. There were no lawmen to pursue them, no wanted posters with their mugs on them. Slocum was the only witness. His shoulder was still tender where their bullet had struck him. Lucky they'd thought they'd killed him that day.

8

Slocum talked to some others around town and learned little else. Midday he rode back to camp with some fresh beef. The storekeeper had butchered beef for several of his customers; most would keep a portion of theirs in an evaporative cooler of wet canvas and cook the rest. The fresh meat should be welcome in his camp. It had been a while since he'd had any, and he liked it lots better than venison.

Wilma looked all fresh, smiling at his arrival when he dropped out of the saddle.

"Got some fresh beef," he said, and she rushed over, excited.

He hitched up his pants and gun, then dug the paper-wrapped meat out of his saddlebags.

"Good and fresh all right," she said, smelling it. "You learn anything?"

"I did. Those killers have got a place out in the badlands with some hot springs."

"Where's that?"

"That's the problem. We're going to have to find it."

She looked him in the eye and winked with a smile. "I bet we can find it."

He agreed and unsaddled his horse, then hobbled him and sent him out to graze. "Reckon I'll shave and take a bath. It's warm enough today."

"That crick ain't warm enough to stay in very long."

"Heat some shaving water for me. And we'll be all clean when we go find those two in the morning."

"Reckon Houston will come along?"

He turned up his hands. No telling what the remittance man would do. Slocum liked him, but Houston had his own world. With a bar of soap in hand, a towel she gave him slung over his shoulder, and a quick kiss, he headed for the stream. The rushing sound of it forewarned him. It would be sharply colder than the sunlight he'd spotted in the clearing.

The water was brisk and quickly shriveled up his sac, but he soaped and rinsed and then went to the sunny spot to dry. *Cold* was not the word. *Damn cold* better described it. On the verge of shaking, he dressed, strapped on his gun belt, and pulled on his socks and boots. Still freezing, he set off in a jog for camp. Goose bumps popped out on his shoulders as he ran into camp.

"Everything all right?" She shaded her eyes to look up at him.

"Cold is all."

She laughed and brushed her shoulder-length brown hair, which shone in the shafts of sunlight. "I warned you. Your shaving water's hot."

He could hardly believe the changes he saw in her from the first day they met. She wore a fresh man's shirt that her large breasts filled out and a divided skirt. No old dirty men's jeans and stained shirt. Her hair glistened with highlights from all the brushing, and her tan complexion looked smooth. Big changes from the ugly witch he'd first laid eyes on. Better said, she had taken some pride in herself. What had she said? Something like he was the first man who had not come home to raw screw her or beat her for screwing up something she had no control over.

He used a hog hair brush and soap to lather up his face,

and using a small mirror, he scraped the whiskers from his cheeks with his sharp, straight-edge razor. The job was soon completed, and she came over and rinsed the rest of the soap off his face with a wet towel.

"What have you done in your life?" She stared hard at him.

"Tried to stay alive and meet pretty women. You're one of them."

She curled her lip in disbelief and impatience. "You had your eyesight checked lately?"

"Nothing wrong with my vision."

She blushed like a young girl and turned away to chew on her lip. "The day I'm pretty, the world will end."

He hugged her shoulder. "Well then, what should we do first?"

"What do you mean?" She frowned hard at him.

"Hell, if the world's going to end, I want to go out in pleasure's arms. You savvy that?"

"Dang right I do." Then she looked around, checking for sight of anyone. Not wasting another second, they were off in a jog, pedaling side by side. He swept up the bedroll. Soon behind the screen of some willows, he began clearing the ground with the side of his boot. Seated on her butt, she heaved off her boots. Then, quick as a cat, she got to her feet and began hanging her clothes on the limber pine branches nearby. Naked as Adam and Eve they hugged and kissed. With the warm wind sweeping over his bare butt, he felt his erection beginning to unfold.

At last with her under him on the blanket, he braced his arms to hold himself over her large treasures and his body positioned between her wide-spread knees. The suggestive wiggling under him raised the bar, and her lips parted in a grin. "Get me!"

He gave her no verbal answer, but his rigid tool soon found her wet gates and slipped inside her like a fine glove. A moan of pleasure escaped her lips and she squeezed him hard against her. His easy pumping opened the way through her ring and soon they were moving like a steam engine out of control—no brakes, racing off a mountain grade. Practically hearing a whistle screaming in his ears, they went faster and faster. The clutches of her inner surfaces her grew spasmodic, and his efforts to plunge into her grew harder and harder until the skin on the swollen head of his dick threatened to explode, and then he came.

Her arms around him tightened, and he felt the rush of her fluids flowing over his balls. They collapsed in a pile, both of them groggy. He tried to recover from the stupor at the whisper of some unseen man close by.

"They must be around here—somewhere. Their saddle horses are here."

Slocum's steady hand drew his .44 from the sheath of leather beside the bedroll. She lay on her stomach, still breathing hard. Her face blanched as she looked at him with an unspoken question. The hammer cocked on his .44 while he lay on his belly behind the willows, he could not see the two men who, from the sounds, were obviously searching for their camp.

"They can't be far."

"His horse is hobbled. I see it out there with the others."

"Where are they?"

Wilma frowned at Slocum as he held out his free hand for her to be still. He wanted to surprise the hell out of them. But first, he needed to be certain how many of them there were. A posse or some bounty hunters—two would be no problem, but three or more individuals could mean the odds were not good enough for him to try to take them.

Seconds went by like minutes or even hours.

"I thought you said this getting him would be easy—"

"Shut up."

They must have passed by and missed Slocum and Wilma in their cozy hiding place. They were centered on Houston's tent. Slocum decided they were farther away. After shaking his head at her offer of his pants, he eased his way through the willows. He could see a pair of men standing in front of Houston's tent, their backs to him.

"Hands in the air or die," Slocum shouted.

"What the hell—?" The older one cocked his hammer, but when he jerked around, Slocum shot him in the chest and he spilled over onto his back. His loaded gun went off in the air, and the second one raised the muzzle of his pistol—obviously shaken by the surprise attack of a naked man—and then a shotgun blast from the side cut him down.

Houston rushed outside, the shotgun butt held tight to his shoulder. "Hey, lad, are you all right?"

Slocum chuckled. "Thanks, they were disturbing my nap."

"I'll check on them if you'd like to dress for the occasion?"

"Handle it. They ain't going anywhere. You know them?"

"No, I have never seen them before. Why did they attack us?"

"They may be hired killers looking for me."

"I must say that business is growing lax if they are. Why, those two couldn't have snuck up on a deaf duck."

"Check them out," Slocum said and went back for his clothing.

In the bright sunlight, Wilma rushed up whispering, "Was that Houston talking?"

Her skirt was on, and she was rapidly tucking her breasts out of sight and buttoning up the shirt. "What will he think? I mean of us being undressed?"

"He'll probably think we were having sex." Slocum buttoned his shirt, then took his pants from her.

"I mean—oh, who in the hell cares, right?"

"For my part, we foiled those two men from killing us. That's all that matters. Act normal. Like we stop killers every day like this."

She laughed and then covered her mouth. With a *no* headshake for his answer, she looked in disbelief at him. When his gun was strapped on, he went over and kissed her, then hugged her shoulder. "We do this all the time."

She elbowed him in the ribs. "Sex, maybe, but not shooting people when you're bare-ass naked."

"Let's go see what we have."

"Fine." She looked to the setting sun for help.

Somberly, he went to where Houston was squatting beside the second gunman. The man nodded, then filled him in. "Says he's Newton. Raddison is the dead man. Says they're horse traders. Wanted to buy our good horses."

Slocum dropped to his knee and took the wounded man's vest in both hands to half raise him off the ground. "You're lying. You came here to kill me. Who hired you?"

"All right. All right. My name's Coleman."

"Who hired you?"

"Jesse did."

"Who's he?"

"Runs a bar in Deadwood." The man shook his head. "I didn't know him. Raddison did. He made the deal."

"For how much?"

"Gave us a three hundred to find and kill you."

"He must have been rich. How did you find me?"

"We paid for all the beer that these two cowboys could drink. Texas ones—we met 'em in a saloon on the road to Cheyenne. Said you was shacking up with some woman up here."

"How did you find us here?"

"Some guy in town said an English guy, some cowboy, and a woman were down here camping on the crick—" He coughed up some blood and then passed out, drowning in his own blood.

"Aye, who would hire killers to find the likes of you?"

"A rich old man whose son came back drunk to a card game and accused me of cheating."

"Money buys killers, doesn't it? Did you meet that pair that they got drunk?"

Slocum made a grim nod. "Once. Their names are Smith and Ward. Those two came by when Wilma was gone to get supplies. They told me that they were looking for Sundance to join his gang. I believe those two robbed and killed their Texas boss after he made a big cattle sale in Montana and they were started back home. He's still missing, best I know."

"So they wanted to join Sundance's outfit, huh?" Houston nodded as if considering the matter.

"You know Sundance? Would he have taken them on?"

"I know some things about him. He's kinda choosy and stays with Mormon help, figures he can trust them better. You know more than that?"

"Yeah, I've met those famous outlaws, Cassidy and Sundance. They came by Wilma's place. Later, Smith and Ward showed up. Those two got caught in a bad storm and I met them when they came to the cabin for shelter. Montana law wants them. It sounds like they got drunk and told those two killers about me being up here."

Houston agreed. "What now?"

"Bury them or feed them to the magpies."

Houston frowned at his answer. "They must have horses nearby. Cowboys never walk far. We'll toss their corpses over them, tie them on, and I will deliver them to some authority," Houston said. "Don't worry, I won't implicate either of you. Now, what are the two of you going to do?"

"Eat some supper," Wilma said. "I've got some good beef to cook."

"Wonderful," Houston said.

"Sounds good," Slocum said. "Tomorrow we're going to look for those two killers out in the badlands. I understand that they have a place out there near some hot springs."

"A vast area. When you come back, look me up."

"We will," Wilma said, and Slocum agreed.

"My dear lady, how unfortunate that you had to be in the midst of all this bloodshed."

"Pard." She shook her head as she was on her knees making a fire. "I've been in lots worse places. Thank you anyway."

"Of course, I imagine you have been. All the same, I regret their imposition on all of us."

"You be careful too," she said. "You two can go find their horses. Going to take me a half hour to get this cooking going."

She made supper while Slocum found and brought in the two horses. Then the two men used the outlaws' bedding to wrap their bodies in. With the corpses laid out, they planned to load them onto the horses in the morning after breakfast.

Houston was shaken by the whole thing when he spoke during supper. "I don't mind taking them to the law, but why would men become killers for such trivial prices?"

Slocum shook his head "No telling. Sounded easy enough. I just appreciate you taking charge of them."

"No problem, chap. It has been rather adventuresome." Houston beamed.

After breakfast the next morning, Slocum and Wilma loaded the two bodies onto their owners' horses and tied them down, then parted with Houston. Slocum watched the Englishman ride off leading the corpse-bearing animals and his mule. Wilma slipped under Slocum's arm to join him. "Now, ain't he a dandy,"

"A real one." Slocum laughed. Houston knew that Slocum had no business messing with the law up there, even if the shooting had been self-defense. The man had done him a big favor handling it and freeing them to go look for the pair of killers. Finding those two would not be easy, but Slocum was sure he'd find someone who knew where they were hiding.

"You know, you could go home and be safe," he said to Wilma as he finished cinching his horse and dropping the stirrup. Jennifer's horse was packed and they were ready to ride off.

"I'd rather rough it with you." She wrinkled her nose at him and grinned.

He smiled at her. Under her weather-beaten felt hat, her face beamed with a freshness and her brushed hair looked bright. No way was she going to be separated from her source of pride: him. With a knowing wink, he nodded that he understood and swung onto his horse. They were off.

The desert beyond Ten Sleep was barren, obviously a much drier land than the Bighorns. Far across this sagebrush desert land lay Yellowstone, the country's federal park and a sacred land to many natives. Still ten nights' sleep away, Slocum had no plans to go see it again. He recalled that the land of steam blowouts, mud pots, and wild game was a great adventure to explore, but he wanted those two killers run down. Someone out in this wasteland would know where they were located.

They found a large flock of sheep and spoke to the shepherd, a scruffy older white man who eyed both of them as if he was suspicious of their interest in him. Slocum understood his fears—sheep people fought lots of opposition from stockmen who claimed that the woolies ruined the range.

"I'm looking for two killers," Slocum said. "One wears a wolf skin cape, and they have a place out here somewhere."

He nodded like he understood. "They came by here a few days ago. I figured they were crazy too. Made me concerned about them killing me for what little I have."

"Deushay and Roberson are their names." Slocum waited for the old man's validation.

"Yes, I met them last year. Their place is somewhere south of here near Red Canyon. You ever been down there?" he asked.

Slocum reined Red around and looked at Wilma. "You ever been there?"

"No." She shook her head.

"Head south." The old man sliced the air with his right arm in that direction. "There's some reddish shades to the rocks. You can't miss them. I'd say they were living in that area."

"Thanks. What can I do for you?"

The old man scratched the shaggy gray hair over his ear. "I don't need nothing. You two be careful. They ain't nice people."

"Thanks for your warning. We'll be careful."

The two of them rode on with little conversation, looking at the ground a lot for signs of fresh tracks. Slocum never felt that they were following any certain trail or tracks. Late in the evening they found a small stream coming from the towering mountains. Wood fuel and even cow pies were both in short supply. He found a dead bush and dragged it in for Wilma to add to their short supply of fuel.

"Thanks," she said. "We'll have enough with that."

He agreed and dismounted. "We still aren't in that red rock area that the old man talked about yet."

She nodded as he undid Red's girth, unsaddled him, and turned him loose to join the other two. Grass was scarce in this land, but the three horses were finding some. Survivors were what he considered them. A fussy horse would never make it in places like this. He'd seen stable horses wilt away in such a cross-country ride. It required a real eager horse, one that wouldn't turn his head away from the available forage, to survive the harsh deserts.

"Think we're going to find them?" She poured him some bubbling coffee into a tin cup.

"I haven't given up. Have you?"

With a glance aside after putting her coffeepot back, she smiled at him. "Hell, I'd go chase boogers with you into never-never land."

He laughed and squatted beside her. "That's what I call loyalty."

Feeling his hand on her shoulder to comfort her, she acknowledged his words, then she rose to use a hook to turn the Dutch oven lid, covered in hot ashes, to more evenly brown her biscuits. A whiff of the sweet sourdough smell attacked his nose when she raised the lid—it would be a great evening.

Later, in the bedroll, he made hard love to her in the gathering coolness of the night. Then crickets set into a serenade for them as they fell asleep. He woke once under the bright stars, turned an ear to any odd sounds, and, satisfied, he went back to sleep till the predawn. In the chill of predawn, he dressed, pulled on his boots, and went to the edge of camp to empty his bladder. Pissing a stream off in the dim light, he heard horses—other than his. He ran for camp and scooped up his rifle.

"What's wrong?" she whispered.

"Horses out in the night."

"Who in the hell are they?"

Then he heard the stallion's scream and laughed. "Mustangs who want to steal the pack mare."

"Horny, huh?" Seated, she laughed, pulling on her boots.

"I guess. Well, we're up. Let's eat and ride some more."

She stood on her toes and kissed him. "Whatever, boss man."

After breakfast, they saddled, packed, and rode out to look for fresh tracks in the golden sun shining on the painted rocks. Crossing a ridge on a much-used trail, he reined up Red. He looked over the country that rolled out before them—they'd found the red rocks.

"Here's the red country," she said, smiling proudly, and reined up beside him.

Disappointed, he shook his head. "A big land to look for them in."

He found several fresh signs and they all came from the east.

"Is that the canyon?" she asked.

"Must be." A deep chasm cut into the rising mountains. Out of the cut, a small stream flowed, then quickly went underground in the sand. No telling about the two killers. They could have been watching Slocum and Wilma ride in, or they could have been sleeping, secure that no one was after them. The clack of the horses' shoes proved loud on the rocks when they began to enter the opening. Some fresher horse apples were strung up the trail and made him satisfied that the killers had either gone up or come down this route.

A few hours later, he smelled smoke. And when he twisted in the saddle, she nodded that she had detected it too. No sign of much here; there were bushy junipers in the canyon and the trail wound through them. A good place to get ambushed. At last the way opened to some grassland. He could see a few hide-covered lodges and the source of the smoke. Out of habit, his hand sought his gun butt.

"What is this?" she asked quietly from behind him.

"Must be a renegade camp. I never heard of any Indians over here until that bartender in Ten Sleep mentioned it."

"Neither have I."

A short old woman came out and shaded her eyes with her hand against the sun's glare to look them over.

He raised his hands in a peace sign and halted his horse. She came toward them, neither friendly nor unfriendly. When she drew closer, he saw she was very old and one of her eyes was stone white. Her buckskin clothing was glazed with dirt and gray with age. The leather looked as fragile as she appeared to be.

"I'm looking for Deushay and Roberson."

"Them motherfuckers gone. I glad," she said.

"I don't blame you. Where did they go?"

"Wellowstone."

"Why there?" he asked, realizing she meant Yellowstone.

"Who knows? Bastards gone. Me glad. You got whiskey? Toothache." She held her hand to her jaw.

Her left eye was a white marble, and he knew many considered such things bad medicine. "No whiskey. Who lives here?"

"Me."

"No others?"

"Sometimes others come hunt sheep."

She meant bighorns—he knew that. "Those two live here sometimes?"

She made a sour face. "Stay sometimes for many moons, then ride away. I like them stay away."

Slocum nodded. "Who else is here?"

Her headshake told him no one. He turned to Wilma. "Let's camp here tonight and we can head for Yellowstone tomorrow. It's a good distance from here."

"Ten plus days, huh?"

"Yes. They might not even be there, and we might not be able to find them. It is a huge place." He shook his head in disappointment.

"Oh, we'll find them. You are too persistent not to."

"Why you want them?" the old lady asked.

"They raped and killed a woman."

She nodded. "Me lucky. They never kill me."

"Holy cow!" Wilma said, sounding upset as she dismounted. "They raped you?"

"Many times."

"They need a lance stuck up their asses." Wilma took his reins and led the horses toward the creek to water them. "They don't deserve to live."

Slocum laughed. Wilma was really boiling. Those worthless tramps raping an old Indian woman. It was a sorry thing, but it had her ire raised up to a hundred twenty degrees. She'd probably stomp around all day over that.

"Where are the hot springs?" he asked the old woman.

"No more," the old woman said with a shrug. "Big roar and rumble and they go dry. Why they went to Wellowstone."

Must have been an earthquake shut them down. "You hear that, Wilma? The hot springs are dry. Why they left, I bet."

"I heard something about why they left." Her hands on her hips, she forced her breasts forward to find some relief for the muscles in her back as the horses drank. He knew what the problem was. His back muscles were the same way—tender. Too much lovemaking at night—but maybe he could stand some more.

The next day they rode northwest, leaving the one-eyed old woman alone in her camp. They left her some coffee and sugar. At a trading post and store they came across the next day, Slocum purchased more supplies to get them to the park. Several families were homesteading along the small river. The storekeeper had seen the two passing by, but they hadn't stopped.

Supplies loaded on the pack mare, Slocum and Wilma rode north across the vast sagebrush sea. It was day two on their trail since leaving the settlement. He'd shot an antelope the day before and had taken the hind quarters. They cooked a big part of it and feasted on it yesterday. The balance would need to be cooked that evening. Days were heating up as the season moved into the hottest part of summer, and the desert was much hotter than the Bighorns' elevation.

Slocum smelled something burning and frowned. "You smelling that smoke?"

"Yes. I wondered what was burning." She put her horse in close to his and twisted around in the saddle, looking for a streak of smoke in the sky.

"North of us." He pointed it out to her. A thin thread stood out against the azure sky.

"Wonder what's making it."

"Probably nothing good." He could read the day or so old tracks of the men they were following. Tracks he'd had his eye on since they left Red Canyon and had been on them since they rode away from the last outpost. One of their horses had thrown a shoe. He imagined it was one of their pack animals, and he'd been watching to see it standing lame near the road.

An hour later, they were looking down from the crest at a burned-out homestead.

"You see anyone?" she asked.

"No one living," he said and booted Red off the ridge. He licked his lower lip. It was slightly crusted from the hot, dry air. What had happened? In this kind of warm weather, homesteads usually didn't burn accidentally.

"You might stay back. This could be grim," he warned her. Those two were no good and might have done something awful to the residents they came across.

"Honey, I've been through enough hell now to make me immune."

"Have it your way." He shrugged. The tracks led right toward the place. He was now even more certain that nothing good had come of the killers' visit to this place.

When he was close enough, he dismounted and handed her the reins to Red. "I'll look around."

She nodded and then dismounted.

Log walls were still smoldering. The roof, which looked

to have been once covered in sod, had caved in. He noted a few articles of small children's clothing on the ground. The smoke was so bad he didn't dare try to enter the fallen-in cabin. Circling the structure, he saw nobody. But the smoky interior worried him more than anything else. The copper smell of blood and a body burning filled his nose at times. Better not tell her.

A few chickens came to see if he had grain for them. She called to him, "Two dogs out here. They've been shot."

"I don't doubt it." He hurried around and saw the two animals lying a few feet apart. One was a shaggy stock dog, the other a hound. They'd been shot several times.

"They do that?" she asked.

"I guess. Those two are the chief suspects. I'm going to the shed over there and see what's inside it."

"I'm coming," she said and hitched the horses to the yard fence.

He was ten feet ahead of her. When he opened the latch and swung open the door on leather hinges, he saw the naked body of a small boy child—likely the one who had worn the clothes—lying on the ground. He turned and caught her before she could see it. "Hold up. You don't want to go in there."

"What's in there?"

"A dead child."

"Those cold-blooded bastards! Why, they're savages."

He hugged her and agreed. The sourness of bile kept rising behind his tongue and he hoped to keep it down. There would be some grisly work for them to do before this day was over.

"How old is that baby?"

"Maybe two or three." He could only guess by its size.

"Then there is probably a baby too. Young wives out here usually have them that close together or closer."

"We need to get hold of ourselves. I wasn't going to tell you, but I am certain now at least another human body is burning up in that cabin."

She hugged him, on the verge of crying. "That is plumb terrible."

"We have a grim day ahead," he said. "Let's bury the child and then maybe the fire will have burned down enough that we can find the other body or bodies inside the cabin."

She used her hand to shade her eyes some and checked the sun time. "Close to midday. Is there a shovel around somewhere?"

"There should be. I'll unsaddle the horses while you look around for one."

She nodded and chewed on her lower lip before she finally spoke again. "I'll look for a blanket or something to wrap the child up in too. This is going to be a tough day. I'm glad you're here and it ain't me alone."

"We can do it." He headed for the horses,

Two hours later, the child was laid to rest. The sandy soil wasn't hard to dig in, and Slocum hoped the boy's body was too deep for the wolves to dig him up. Wilma fixed some food. He tied a wet kerchief over his mouth so he could get close enough to toss water on the smoking logs and find the half-burned corpse of a man in the house. With no way to recognize him, Slocum wrapped his remains in one of his own blankets and dreaded the work still ahead.

"We better eat something," Wilma said, bringing him some fresh coffee.

He sat cross-legged on the ground and tried to get the dead stench out of his nose and the taste of smoke out of his mouth. The coffee made him salivate, which was better tasting anyway. He needed to apprehend those two killers before they slaughtered any more innocent people. Madmen. Had there been a woman here? He thought there probably had been. What had happened to that poor soul? He really didn't want to know.

After sundown, he finished covering up the man's corpse with dirt in the second grave he'd dug. His hands ached and his back felt the same, but the job was done. He went down to the small river and tried to wash away the remains of the distasteful duty he'd just performed that saturated his very body. Wilma dried him off when he came out.

"I have some supper ready, if you can eat."

"I'll try." He really felt as done in physically and mentally as he could ever recall. Even his shoulder wound complained. At times while he was fighting in the Civil War, he could recall being so exhausted that he couldn't even sleep when he did get a chance. His skin crawled under his shirt.

The next morning, they left the homestead and traveled on northwest. Days dragged out into longer hot ones. Their water sources became poorer and alkali-bitter tasting. They reached the Gray Horn River—or at least he thought that was the name of the one that flowed out of the mountains coming from the still-distant Yellowstone.

He dropped out of the saddle and discovered that the river tasted much better than the springs and streams they'd been coming across. Wiping his mouth on his sleeve, he nodded at her. "We're still days from Yellowstone, but at least the water's better."

She smiled, weary-looking, and dismounted. Then she laughed. "It may be a long way yet to hell, but we now have good drinking water, huh?"

He laughed too. "Right on, gal. Hell, I may stop and take a bath. The water looks so damn inviting."

"That might not be a bad diversion." She went to unbuttoning her shirt.

"You better rebutton that shirt. We're getting company."

She started to do so and frowned. "Who's coming?"

"A passel of Injuns." He stepped over to Red and jerked out his Winchester. By then they could hear them ki-yacking like coyotes as they short loped toward them.

"I'll be gawdamned. Rode this far and going to be scalped by some bucks." She shook her head in dismay.

His eyes narrowed. His hands tightened on the stock and forearm of the rifle. That wouldn't happen before he took a few of them with him.

9

The leader wore a long-tailed, feathered war bonnet. He held up his rifle and the whole war party shut down, and then they spread out in a line. The war-painted bucks with rifles across their laps, some armed with bows, sat their multicolored ponies; all stared at Slocum and Wilma with the hard eyes of hawks. If Slocum was going to die beside this sweet water stream, it was better than being beside an alkali pothole.

He held up his right hand in peace. Then whispered to her, "Here goes."

She nodded, obviously thinking, as he did, that this meeting could turn fatal. The chief said something to a young man, who rode forward from the line until he was just a few feet from Slocum and Wilma.

"My name is Blue Horse."

"Slocum is mine, and this is Wilma."

"We are looking for two white men and a woman. The men raped a teenager and left her for dead."

"Did one have a wolf skin cape?"

The boy nodded and some surprise showed in his dark eyes, then they leveled out. "You know them?"

"They were headed for Yellowstone, last we heard. If they

didn't go there, they are circling back. I think the woman with them is the wife of a homesteader that they killed."

He nodded. "I will go tell my chief."

With his pony whirled around, he raced back and began speaking to the one under the war bonnet. The man nodded as he talked. Blue Horse charged back and slid his horse to a stop. "You are certain about them?"

"Yes. They killed a woman in the Bighorns. We're on their trail too."

"We thought we'd find their camp by backtracking them."

Slocum shook his head. "The hot springs they once had back there went dry. They are going to Yellowstone to be treated."

"I will tell my chief." He rode back and conversed again with his leader.

"They don't want us, then, do they?" she whispered.

"Hell if I know, but I think we can breathe easier for now."

"Good. Where are they from?"

"I think they're Wind River people. They ain't Sioux or Cheyenne. They'd already have killed us if they were on the war path."

"Good to know."

The boy came back. "My chief thanks you and your wife. Go in peace, we will follow them that way."

"Be best," he said and then waved to the chief. The leader waved back and turned his string of bucks, and they left in a loud chorus of war cries.

"Wait a minute," she said. "I have to pee. That was too close for my comfort."

He agreed and looked to the sky to thank his maker. Way too close. Now those worthless ones had more enemies. Who was the woman with them? He'd been reading her barefoot tracks since they'd left the site of the fire. Was she the dead man's wife and mother of the baby? In time he might learn—sad deal piled on more sad deals. He'd be glad when this entire situation was settled.

They came across some white settlers as they drew closer

to the gates of Yellowstone. Not exactly gates—there was a single-way path that scaled the eastern wall and led over the top and eventually to the great falls on the Yellowstone River. Midday, a rider on horseback met them.

He was a man in his thirties, bearded, wore a threadbare suit coat and flat-brim black hat, and looked like a preacher. "Good morning, ma'am, and to you too, sir."

"Same to you," Slocum said.

"Heading to hell, I guess?"

"We're going west. Is it that bad?" Slocum asked.

"Oh, yes, that settlement back there is full of fornicators, loose-moraled women, drunken louts, and blasphemous individuals—excuse me, ma'am. But it surely is a place that should be avoided should God desire to turn them into salt like the Bible said."

"We're tracking two killers. So are the Indians."

"I talked to those savages. They are not doing God's will either, though they profess to be Christian converts. May thunder strike all the fake Christians dead who wander upon this earth. Is this woman your married wife?"

Slocum shook his head.

"Then when you hear the thunder on the mountains, you will know it is God seeking to kill you for your blasphemy, sir. Good day, I can only pray for your redemption." He booted his horse and left them.

"Why did you tell him we weren't married? It would have saved him the pain of having to pray for us too." She bent over in laughter, about to fall out of the saddle.

"I hate those 'we're all going to hell' preachers. I have a different concept of who my Maker is." He shook his head. "I bet we're alive today because some godly messenger showed them Wind River people who we were as people."

She agreed and they rode on. No sign of the Indians; they must have avoided the small settlement they found at the foot of the mountain. One man called it Hooter, but Slocum was never certain of the real name and didn't care. They added some more supplies to their panniers at a log-cabin general store before riding on. He also bought some catgut line and iron hooks to add to his things, promising Wilma some fresh trout.

No one in that village had seen the two men pass by, or so they said when he asked about them—obviously they'd avoided leaving any sign at the settlement. But several miles up in the canyon in a broad valley they met a whiskered man on the road. He said his name was John Jeffers, and after Slocum talked to him about the two killers and the woman with them he nodded.

"That woman is with Martha, my wife, right now. Her name is Gina, and she's near out of her mind."

"You left them at your place. The woman?"

"Yes, why?"

"They are ruthless men, and if this Gina ran away from them and they're looking for her, they may kill your wife."

"I never thought about that."

"Here, Wilma, you bring the packhorse and come slower. We're going fast right back to his place. You can follow us."

She nodded grimly. "Go do what you must do. I'll be a-coming."

"My heavens, I never thought of that," Jeffers said again as they galloped their horses westward.

When Slocum and Jeffers arrived at the man's claim, his prematurely gray-headed wife came rushing out of the front door. "John, oh, John, those grubby men kidnapped Gina again and left not fifteen minutes after you left here. They caught that poor woman bringing me a pail of water to the house. There was nothing I could do."

"It's all right now, darling." He hugged her and shook his head at Slocum. "I should have known them bastards would come back looking for her. Poor girl is out of her mind."

"They're ruthless. They murdered her child and husband and set her cabin on fire. We buried them two a few days ago. Plus they murdered a rancher's wife up in the Bighorns. That's why we're after them."

"They can't get far. We can track them," Jeffers said.

"We better not leave your wife here alone. There's some Indians after them too. But if they double back on us—"

Wilma arrived and, dismounting, she hurried over. "Where is she?"

"They came back and got her. Mrs. Jeffers can tell you all about her."

"Well, gawdamn! You mean we got here too late?" Wilma stomped her boot in the dust.

Slocum, who had dismounted, nodded. "They're headed up into the mountain, near as we can tell."

"What are we going to do about it?" Wilma asked.

"If they know we're looking for them, it may spook them and they'd be even harder to track. I say give them a day. I don't know about the Indians looking for them."

"Oh—" She chewed on her lower lip. "What about the woman? Their captive."

Slocum hugged Wilma to his chest. "That damn narrow trail will take a good half day to climb to the top, maybe more. We could be ambushed if they discover we're coming up it."

"He's right, lady," Jeffers broke in. "It would be foolish not to let them think they're getting away. That trail is steep and in the open most of the way. You don't want to meet any ambushers on that path."

About to cry, Wilma shook her head. "I just can't help it. That poor woman has to be in a living hell."

"Besides, our horses are near done in. Look at them. They look like gutted greyhounds." Slocum slumped his shoulders and shook his head.

"My name's Martha. The men can put up the horses. Come along with me," she said to Wilma.

"I'm—" She sniffed. "I'm Wilma—thanks."

"Good to meet you. I don't get much female company. My, your hair looks so pretty. How do you keep it looking so nice—traveling, I mean?"

"It ain't easy." Wilma nodded at Slocum and went on to the house with Martha.

Slocum kept glancing up at the mountain towering above them as they unsaddled and unpacked the horses. Where had those two gone? No doubt upward over the top. If he hadn't had Wilma with him, he'd have ridden on, regardless of how tired his animals were, and when they couldn't go a foot farther, he'd set into walking them down. But he had to think about Wilma—and let their ponies rest. The grass looked strong in this valley.

This whole episode kept taking turns he never expected. His plan had started out simple—catch those two and make them pay for murdering Jennifer. Instead he'd worn his butt out riding, looking for tracks that disappeared and then finding them again along with more tragedy that those men had caused. *God, help me find them, please.*

10

A strong storm blew in and they stayed another day at Jeffers's place. The couple had moved to this location from Wisconsin. They had considerable garden produce to feed them through the winter. Root crops still growing, like potatoes and turnips, would be kept in their good cellar, and Jeffers had started work on a fuel supply of wood. A very precise man, he and his wife had no fears about severe weather and a long winter.

"We're a lot better prepared than last year," Jeffers said. "I trapped all winter and that saved us the first year. I sold several hides last spring." He smiled. "And that's why we can afford to have coffee."

"This a better place than Wisconsin?"

"Oh, yes. The trapping outside of the park is untouched. We ate elk meat all winter."

"How many times have you been up on top?" Slocum asked.

"Oh, several times. It's steep and narrow. You were smart to wait out the storm. One thing they don't have in Wisconsin is mountains." He laughed and puffed on his pipe. "Yes, we

95

like it up here. I'll dry several trout too this fall to eat next winter."

The next day the sun was well up, the sky was clear, and the wind coming out of the north was cold. They pulled out for the way up into Yellowstone, a great plateau. No need for Slocum to ask Wilma if she wanted to stay with the Jeffers. She was bundled up and mounted early, and they left west-ward bound. He felt certain that they had some clear days ahead, since the heavy storms had gone on east.

Midmorning, they hit the trailhead and started up the grade. There were official signs warning people they were enter-ing the Yellowstone National Park: No commercial hunting or trapping allowed. Federal authority will prosecute any violators.

The trail went up like a staircase. The way soon narrowed to a single path that clung to the mountainside and looked over lots of land far below them.

"Times like this I could use some eagle wings," Wilma said from behind him.

Slocum agreed. So far, so good, but he knew her fear of heights from Bighorn Canyon. This way soared higher than that. Traces of snow from the storm yesterday soon showed, and he wished he'd waited another day for it to melt. One misstep by a horse could mean death at the bottom of the cliff. His stomach curdled and he felt light-headed; some-times high elevations got to him. This day he needed no such thing to happen. The drums in his ears felt pin sharp.

Three hours later they pulled out on top, and he rode a short way across the lightly snow-crusted meadow, then dropped out of the saddle, holding the horn to get his bear-ings and legs under him.

"Stay on the horse," he shouted at Wilma. "I'll help you down as soon as I get my own legs working."

She pushed her horse up close to him. "Damn, that's a big lake, ain't it?"

He couldn't think of the name of the wide expanse of clear blue water nearby, but she was right. It was a large lake that stretched away from them. After a minute or two, he went over and helped her down. Then they staggered over to a large downed tree and cleared off the crust of thin snow so they could sit upon it.

"Thank God," she said. "That was the worst haul up here yet."

"We're here and we're fine." He clapped the top of her leg beside him. "Us and those horses need some rest."

"Oh, yes, we do. I'm just so glad we had some rest before we tried coming up here."

"I knew it would be rough."

"Where did they go from here?"

"I'd say the steam pots and the geyser fields."

"How far is that away from here?"

"A two- or three-day ride from here."

She nodded. "Damn, Slocum, I wish we'd met years ago. I'd never come up here with anyone else. I can see from here though why the government made it a federal park."

"You ain't seen nothing yet, sister. Right over there I can see a lean-to shelter someone built that we can use tonight to sleep under. Don't look like rain, but it will get cold as hell tonight. That lean-to reflecting a campfire's heat would be nice."

"I'm with you." She hugged his arm. "Isn't your butt getting cold sitting on this snowy log?"

"I was treating my piles."

She gave him a shove and laughed. "Let's make camp and build a fire."

"You bet." Stiff from the ride up, he walked out some of the stiffness gathering firewood.

The horses were unsaddled, unpacked, hobbled, and turned loose to graze. The sun's midday power began to melt the light coating of snow as they gathered fuel. Bald eagles screamed at Slocum and Wilma, invaders to their land. A brilliant day in the nation's first park. He liked it.

In the lean-to, reroofed with new boughs of pine, they sat together with the radiant heat of their fire warming them.

"Could we stay up here forever?" she asked, busy brushing her hair.

He reached over and twisted her face toward him so he could kiss her. She quit brushing and threw her arms around his neck. The passion between them sparked more needs, and like honeymooners, they were soon in a race to see who could get naked first and under the covers. At last in each other's arms with him on top, their bare skin had cooled enough to make her shiver and snuggle. Breath caught up, they sought each other like starving wolves under the covers.

His erection quickly swelled tight. Her hand directed him inside, and she threw her head back, savoring his entry with a sharp cry. This was a fiery match, with her hunching into his driving thrusts and both of them absorbed in the total process, seeking that pleasure that would send them soaring with eagles above the lake. Her sheath tightened on his invading penis. The way grew more difficult for him to plunge in and out. The tight skin on the head of his dick felt like it was being rubbed raw with each stroke.

Then, lying on top of her boobs, he reached under her, clutched the cheeks of her hard-muscled ass, and drove to the deepest part of her to signal his impending cannon fire. The long explosion caused both of them to catch their breath and savor the moment of truth that drained them.

She snuggled against him and shook her head. "Mind if I say thanks?"

He smiled down at her and shook his head. "It's been my pleasure."

"Where will we go tomorrow?"

"We need to move toward the geyser basin. If Deushay and Roberson want heated treatment, that's where they'll head."

"Is that the only place to find it?" she asked.

"No, there're all kinds of places where heated water escapes hell up here, but the basin has the most. And it's a good ways across these mountains."

"Several days?"

He nodded, wondering about their captive, Gina. That poor woman must be desperate by this time with no hope of ever being rescued.

11

They went by the Grand Canyon of the Yellowstone, and he showed her the high falls heading up to its source. He also took her to see the other turbulent falls above that one. Across the shallow river flowing out of Yellowstone Lake, they met an army captain, John Hightower, who was set up in log quarters. The officer came out on the porch and met them very formally.

"We are chasing two killers who have a woman hostage," Slocum explained.

"Private," Hightower said to his aid, "send for Sergeant Malloy." He turned back to Slocum.

"If they're in the park, no doubt some of my men have seen them. Come into my office. Missus—"

"I'm Wilma, and this is Slocum. Nice to meet you, sir."

"My pleasure, indeed, and you too, sir."

Slocum thanked him, looking along the vast lakeshore for any sign of the men they sought. It didn't surprise him that the pair of killers had avoided the outpost, especially with a hostage woman. Somehow they must be more familiar with the park's layout than Slocum had expected—no problem; it was vast land. A year or two after the Lewis and Clark Expedition, John Colter had slipped into this boiling steam pot land, and from his descriptions, people started calling it Colter's Hell. Many thought the simple trapper had gone crazy, talking about quarter-mile-high-spewing geysers that went off regularly like clockwork. But Colter had gone back up there with the first fur trappers, and after a narrow escape from some angry Blackfeet, went back down the Missouri and farmed for the rest of his life. By then people had heard the truth—there was a hell up there.

Slocum and Wilma took supper with Captain Hightower. Slocum could tell she was impressed with the style of the meal and even the crystal glasses the champagne was served in. Later under the covers in the guest cabin provided to them, Wilma stretched out naked beside Slocum.

"My, you have such good friends," she teased, overcome by the luxury.

"Now, don't get carried away. We still have a mission, or I do."

"Darling, I am just enjoying a moment in the finer ways of life. My first experience with boys was me belly down over a barrel. It became rougher from there on."

"You did have it rough, then."

"Lord, I told you I was a tomboy growing up and not much of a lady. But things, and bodies, change. I started getting boobs, and then boys stopped looking at me like I was some fence post. Me, I didn't notice until more and more of them hugged me every chance they got. Then Harold Carnes kissed me one moonlit night when just the two of us were skinny dipping, and I wondered, what the hell was that for?"

Slocum chuckled and hugged her "Well?"

"Me? I also noticed his usual soft-looking pecker was upright like a barber pole and poking me in the belly."

"What happened next?"

"Oh, he made an attempt to put it in me. The two of us standing up. That didn't work and we both fell down laughing. He was a smooth talker and said if I'd get belly down on a wooden barrel, he'd show me how folks did it."

"And so you laid on one?"

"Of course, I was dumb and about trembling. There was an old barrel back of the barn, and we snuck up there. Didn't have any clothes on. I got on the barrel and he came from behind. He first wanted to use my ass, but I knew that would never work. And finally he found about two inches of his erection he could poke in me.

"That first experience must have really inflated his ego. Two nights later he was back for more. He wasn't much better at his business. He was neither flattering nor did he show any compassion for me—so I told him we would not do it again."

"What did he do then?"

"Tried to bribe me. Tried to make me believe he loved me." She shook her head, casually rubbing the muscles in Slocum's corded stomach. "No end of what he tried. So I thought that was over. But he brought two of his buddies, and they caught me out of the house. He said if I screamed, he'd tell my mother I'd been screwing him all the time. Boy, I was really being blackmailed.

"He scared me enough, I had to cooperate. He removed my overalls and my flour sack underwear, and he had them other two hold me belly down across the barrel. He couldn't do much more than before. On and off. Maybe got inside me an inch and he came. But my heart sank when that Whitlow boy got back there. He was no stranger to sticking it to women, I quickly learned. He whipped out his dick and jacked it up, and so when he parted my legs, my heart stopped. Talk about a poker—he came on like a stud horse and drove his hard pecker all the way inside. I about fainted after he used me. Then Sherman Grange must have taken lessons from Whitlow, 'cause he came on hard and deep too.

"I went to bed that night feeling dirty and knowing I'd lost my virginity for nothing. But I swore anyone after that would pay dear for my body."

"You first husband treat you all right?"

"Oh, he was drunk on our wedding night and barely did

much. Didn't matter 'cause by then I didn't expect much."

Her hand was jacking Slocum off. Aroused, he lifted the covers and climbed between her legs, which were parted in a V. She put him inside her gates, then scooted down to be under him.

He kissed her and then drove himself deep inside. In the morning, they'd have to leave these comfortable quarters, but for now he pounded her into the whirlpool of their sexual experience.

Two days later, Slocum and Wilma were coming up the stream west of the geyser basin. Hot springs flowed, steaming, into the cold river. They had ridden around many boiling pot fields, and steam spewed out of geysers into the sky. Wilma, obviously awed, twisted her head around to see all that she could.

"That big one should go off anytime now," he told her, twisted in the saddle.

"You seen any sign of them?" she asked.

He shook his head. Not in days. Several times he'd come across tracks and grown excited, but they faded or proved to be nothing. Instinct had driven him to this basin, though he had begun to wonder if all his intuition was running out without any evidence as to their whereabouts.

"Are there any more army men up here?" she asked.

"Hightower said there was a company of men up here."

"Where are they at?"

"Somewhere near the big geyser, I'd guess."

"I haven't seen any."

"They might be out patrolling."

She agreed and they rode on up the valley past more fields of bubbling mud pits. Soon the army tents were visible on the right, and he pointed them out to her. In response she smiled. "I don't see any cabins."

He nodded and they rode on. The army up here probably didn't have any more special cabins like that one they had stayed in at Captain Hightower's camp. Feeling downhearted about his nonsuccess, Slocum finally dropped off his saddle and stretched his back. It was a warm day. Then Wilma shouted, "Look quick. It's blowing up."

He turned in time to see the steam and water go eighty feet high. Impressive sight. He wondered what Colter had thought at his first viewing of the explosion.

"Army's coming," she said softly.

"Welcome to Yellowstone, folks," the sergeant said, strolling up to them.

"Good afternoon." Slocum nodded to the burly man.

"First time here?"

"Not for me, but it's Wilma's first."

"I'm Sergeant Copper. Can I do anything for you?"

"We talked to Captain Hightower over at the falls. There are two men who kidnapped a woman out east in Wyoming who supposedly are up here taking baths. They murdered Wilma's neighbor over in the Bighorns. We've been tracking them off and on for several weeks."

"What do they look like? Maybe I've seen them."

"One wears a wolf skin cape. They don't bathe—"

"They were here two days. Told me that the woman with them was one of them's wife."

"She even coherent by this time?"

"I thought something was wrong with her. But I figured only a crazy woman would marry the likes of either of them."

Slocum agreed. "Where were they going?"

"Willoughby Springs."

"Where in the Sam Hill is that?" Slocum looked around. He had more tracking to do.

"A couple days' ride to the east."

"Why there?"

"Special place to take baths. Indians use it all the time. And it won't cook you to death either."

"We get a little rest, we'll go find them. Right, Wilma?"

"Yes, and thanks, Sergeant," she said.

"I'll send a few of my men along with you. We don't need

killers in the park. I really wondered about that little woman."

Wilma rode in closer. "They killed her husband and baby. We buried them."

Slocum felt better. They were in the region and he was close. This whole thing might wind up soon. And it better. They were quickly running out of supplies, and there were no settlements nearby where they could buy any more.

"Put your horses in our trap," the sergeant said. "Lots of damn bears up here. We'll guard them with ours." He turned to Wilma. "Ma'am, we don't have any facilities like my captain has for guests, but we have got some wall tents. Would you two sleep in one tonight?"

"We sure will. Thank you," she said and smiled at Slocum.

They feasted on elk steaks that evening and at last sat alone in the tent. She was on his lap and holding him tight. "We'll get them. We're close. The army will help you."

He kissed her and agreed. They were close enough. It might happen.

12

Dawn was mountain cool in the valley of the geysers. Sergeant Copper assigned two men to go with them: Private Ned Klein and Corporal Telman Davis. Ned was tall and thin, his partner Telman short with a bulldog build. Both men seemed pleased at their assignment and were ready to go in the early morning. Each of them armed with a revolver and repeating rifle, they looked like veterans at the park patrol business.

Slocum asked the corporal to lead the way since he outranked the other soldier. Telman agreed to do that, and they rode out. The army pair had a loaded mule bearing their camp gear, and Wilma led Jennifer's horse, which bore their personal things. Once out of the valley of the geysers, they spread out in a single line, heading eastward on a worn trail for the site where they hoped to find the murderers.

"How long have you two been on their trail?" Telman asked as they rode along.

Slocum looked back at Wilma for her answer. She shook her head at first. "I've lost track. We've been on their trail for weeks, I think. Originally we had a remittance man helping us find them, but after we had a shooting scrap with some

106

other outlaws, he took their bodies to the law and we went on. That's been about three weeks ago."

Telman shook his head. "You two are sure determined."

"The lady they murdered was very generous. There was no reason to kill her," Slocum said.

"Who is the woman with them?" Ned asked.

"A woman they kidnapped from her homestead. We buried her child and husband several days ago."

Ned nodded and turned back to look at them. "I thought she was some kind of a white slave."

"Her name is Gina. She escaped them once," Slocum said, "but they came back and kidnapped her again before we could stop them."

"What will you do when you capture these men?"

"I guess I'll save that until we catch them." Slocum wasn't telling them his real intentions: to send them both to hell. The military may have given Ned and Telman orders on what to do.

Ned nodded and went on.

"Willoughby Springs many miles from here?" Slocum asked.

"Maybe twenty," Telman said and shared a nod with him.

"That ain't far," Wilma echoed. "We've already been to hell and back."

Slocum reined up beside her and clapped her on the leg. "I never asked if you were all right this morning."

"Hell, I'm super fine riding anywhere with you."

"Good. I knew better than ask if you wanted to wait in camp for our return."

"No way. No way you could do that to me."

He nodded. "Nice to have two professionals tracking for us and knowing where we're going."

She agreed and let him in line ahead of her.

In the afternoon they reached a point Ned thought was halfway to the springs, and they made camp. He drew a map in the dirt of the junction of some streams that they would find around noon the next day. Slocum thanked him, and they grained their horses before hobbling them.

"We close enough for them to smell our campfire?" Slocum asked.

Ned checked with Telman, then they shook their heads. "No. We're far enough away."

Slocum was satisfied. He busted up wood to burn, and the two soldiers brought him more from the surrounding area. Wilma planned to make some Dutch oven biscuits and work on a large evening meal. Noisy camp robbers fussed at them. A screaming bald eagle came floating down the canyon like some kind of harbinger warning of peril nearby. Slocum wasn't certain of anything being wrong, but the skin crawled on the back of his neck at the bird's shrill screaming.

They ate Wilma's meal, and the two soldiers bragged on her cooking. She beamed. Then they set up a guard schedule, just in case. Slocum had the middle shift. When he replaced Ned, the stars were sparkling above the evergreen-forested canyon walls.

"Hear anything?" Slocum asked the soldier.

"No. Nothing out of the ordinary. Shout if you need backing. I'd rather be woken up than kilt in my sleep."

"I agree." Rifle across his lap and his back to a tree trunk, Slocum sat above the camp and breathed in the evergreen-scented air and took his place as guard. Night sounds kept him listening. Then he heard horses coming—Indians. He shook both soldiers and told them to be quiet. Then he awoke Wilma and gave her his .44. "Be quiet. We have company coming."

"All right."

The two soldiers gathered all their horses and hid them up the hillside in the woods. Then they took up defensive positions behind some huge fallen trees. Slocum knelt down and wondered who the Indians were. Some had dismounted and were checking the campsite. Lots of talking in guttural words that made no sense to Slocum. He doubted they'd simply leave and go on. The camp was fresh. Panniers and saddles all around, they had to know that someone was nearby. He had his rifle sight on the silhouette of a feather headdress–wearing buck busily going through their campsite in the starry light and kicking an empty bedroll.

Hammer cocked back on his rifle, Slocum could knock him down easily with the first shot. But there were several of them moving in and out of the shadows. If he shot one, they'd sure have to fight the rest.

The other two men were too far away to whisper at.

"Soldiers! We are friends!" someone shouted in English.

"What the hell does that mean?" he hissed at them.

"They must be friendly," Telman said.

"Who are you?" Ned shouted.

"We are from Big Thunder's camp."

"They're—from Wind River. I know them," Telman said. "Hold your fire, I am coming."

"Be careful," Slocum said.

"I will, but they're friendly."

"Good."

The soldier set out holding his rifle over his chest. Slocum waited. Ned joined him with his own long gun in hand. "He knows them."

"What was friendly yesterday might not be today," Slocum said, still suspicious.

"I know, but he's well known by most of the friendly tribes that come up here."

"Are we going to be scalped or not?" Wilma asked quietly, joining them.

"Wait and see," Slocum said.

In a short while, Telman told them it was all right to come down. Still not satisfied, Slocum helped her over the log.

"They're after those two killers too," Telman said on his arrival. "The sergeant back at camp told them we were up here looking for them also."

"I met them before we came up in the park," Slocum said, recognizing some of them as they built up the fire.

They all sat in a circle in the orange light of the flames.

Telman talked through the Indian boy who interpreted. There were nine total in the war party. Most were young men armed with an assortment of arms, from muzzleloaders to repeaters.

They had had to go back home and get supplies, which was why they were so late catching up. That made sense. Slocum settled some with that knowledge. He shared a nod of approval with Wilma to ease her concern. After they spoke for some time, the leader of the party, Big Knife, said he wanted to send two scouts ahead to locate the killers. Telman turned to Slocum to ask what he thought about that idea.

"Don't let them see you," he said to the boy. Translated, they agreed. Slocum told them good night. He and Wilma took their bedroll and went up the hillside to be alone.

"Think they'll kill us in our sleep?" She was under the covers with her back raised up for her to work her dress up past her hips. "I would rather die satisfied."

On his knees, he crossed over her legs, and she opened them in a V for him. "So would I."

Carefully, he lowered himself down and kissed her before he plunged his erection into her. She gave a sigh. "Oh, I never missed it as bad as I do these nights. I think I may go crazy without you."

He eased his growing tool inside her and then began to work her over. The skintight head of his dick pressed deeper and deeper. The viselike contractions inside her added to his excitement and growing pleasure. Soon he was going to the bottom of her and she raised her ass to meet his freight train–like thrusts. They began to fly through the mountaintops, soaring over the snowcapped peaks. Then he felt the rise of his semen and gave his load a hard push. She collapsed, clutching him. He kissed her face and she went limp.

Maybe they could sleep after that. They did.

At dawn, Wilma made the men food and they packed up. The two Indian scouts had not come back, so the whole party went looking for them. They wound up the narrow canyon and finally crossed over one pass. Near midday, Telman pointed to a cleft in the mountains far ahead. "That's where they should be."

"I wonder why the scouts aren't back." Slocum said to him.

"Strange. He sent good men."

"I'm beginning to think something happened to them."

"I don't know, but you're right, they should be back by now."

Slocum booted Red up beside the soldier. "Those two've lived on their wits, I think, for a long time. They've killed several people since we began trailing them. The worst thing of all is the poor white woman they hold in slavery."

The party held up at midday. Telman and an Indian scout were going ahead to see what they could learn. Slocum told the rest not to build any fires. There was grass in the clearing for their horses to graze. So they sat back to wait. Slocum had told Telman to be careful—those men were killers. Not satisfied, he walked back and forth, wishing he'd gone with them.

In a half hour, the buck who had gone with Telman was back on a lathered horse. The translator said the two killers were gone and the other two scouts they'd sent the night before had been murdered.

"Is the woman with them?" Slocum asked the boy. No one knew.

"You were right," Wilma said, hugging his arm as they went for their horses.

Being right wasn't his goal. He wanted to prevent more people dying. But he hadn't and he blamed himself for the losses. Even as he caught Red and gathered in the pack-horse's lead rope, he decided the two of them might be at the end of their chase. Their supplies were seriously low, and he couldn't risk taking Wilma farther into the wilderness. The idea of giving up rasped at his conscience, but some things in life were impossible.

In two hours, they were all in the camp that the killers used. Slocum had gone to view two corpses. The scouts had been brutally slaughtered. No sign of the poor woman hostage anywhere. They had gone on and Telman was sitting on a log holding his head.

"I thought we could get them," he said.

"They're madmen," Slocum said. "You can't think like they do. I've been tracking them for over six weeks."

"What should we do?"

"Go back. I'm going to take her home."

"I don't blame you. We'll watch for them. Maybe the Indians will take up their tracks."

Slocum agreed, but he doubted they would. They acted more crestfallen over their losses than he was over the whole matter.

"You're down at the heels," Wilma said, bringing him a cup of fresh coffee.

"I've got reasons. Our supplies are too low to go on. There is no place out here to replenish our needs. Obviously they could go on for months and miles. We're at the end of that rope."

"Only so much you can do. I understand. What's next?"

"We can drop south, get out of the park, and work our way back to the Bighorns."

She agreed with a sober look. "I don't know what else we can do."

"I know something we can do." He winked at her mischievously.

"Well, there's always that." She laughed.

He hugged her shoulder. "Time to call it quits."

"Yes."

He looked at the forested mountains that hemmed them in. The ride home would be a long one. God be with that poor woman that they had. That pain stabbed his heart.

13

He changed his plans, feeling it was better for them to go out the east gate. They bought some supplies from the government outpost at Geyser Park. Then they wound their way eastward after deciding the route back to the east gate would be their best way out. They visited Captain Hightower for a night, then surveyed the great falls again, passed through the buffalo herds, and at last came off the mountain. The breathtaking descent to the valley below left Wilma so shaken that at the bottom, he had to set her down on a blanket. He made her take off her britches and then he rubbed the circulation back into her bare legs.

This workup led to an amorous session in the bedroll between them. But he was relieved to be off the mountain and down at the base again. They spent the rest of the day resting around their camp.

The next day, they traveled from the base and stayed over for one night at the homestead with the Wisconsin couple, Martha and John Jeffers, who were sad to know that despite their efforts, the young woman had not been rescued. But Jeffers said no one could question their efforts to find her.

On the move, Slocum and Wilma did not stop at the

113

burned-out homestead and instead swept across the inner desert for Ten Sleep in six hard-pushed days. Stopping at Farr's General Store, he asked after the whereabouts of the remittance man, Houston.

"He was in here a few days ago," the clerk said. "I guess he went back up the canyon to his base camp."

Slocum thanked him and bought a few supplies and some candy. Then they used the store's campsite on the stream. Busy fixing them some supper over the campfire, Wilma rose and shook her head. "If I have to go over that damn canyon trail again, I'll stay up on top until I die."

"Quit dreading it." He got up and grasped her around the waist from behind. He found her tickle points. Soon his efforts began to work, and she was laughing and shouting for him to quit. He turned her around to face him and smothered her with kisses. When his tongue slipped into her mouth to tease her some more, her eyes flew open in shock.

"The food will burn."

"Set it off the grill. We have more important things to do."

"Oh, my God. You're serious." She slipped out of his hold, knelt down to put the pans off the fire, and stood up, unbuttoning her blouse. He had his boots toed off and set his gun belt on the ground close to the bedroll they'd already laid out. She pushed the pants off her hips, and her white skin shone in the afternoon sun filtering down through the cottonwoods.

Both naked as Adam and Eve under the covers, Slocum was on top of her, eating up her right breast and his tongue teasing the large nipple until it grew stiff as a nail. She was shifting around, trying to get the growing erection directed inside her slit. At last she drove both of her hands under him and stuck his rod through her wet gates. She raised her butt off the ground and hugged him to her thick breasts.

"Oh, Gawd, that feels better than ever," she whispered in his ear.

The head of his dick was stretched so tight by then, he decided it might split and explode. His butt made the drive in and out as her vise began to grasp him tighter and tighter. She was puffing for air and so was he, his balls slapping her ass with every stroke. He knew she was wild with desire for more and more, and he intended to give her all that he could. The going went harder, the friction tougher, and the pain increased in his hips and the head of his dick. But he was going to completely take her over the mountains and make her faint.

Her breathing grew louder. Her efforts to meet him were sapping her strength, but she was on a wild path to get everything that he had. He wanted her loop-legged when he finished with her. Then she cried out and he speeded up. The flow from her ran out in the narrowest space between his pistonlike dick and her walls. Then the knot in the end of his dick exploded, and she fainted to lie limp under him. He braced himself up, resting only on her muscled belly. One thing he noticed, she'd gotten in great physical shape in the course of making their long odyssey.

With her fingers, she parted the hair in her face and shook her head. "You could make any woman forget her name," she whispered. "I'll make it over the trail 'cause I know there's another side up there."

She clamped her legs together and squeezed his dick tight inside her vise. "You want supper?"

He punched his dick into her deeper, and she gasped for her breath. "Lord sakes, are we doing it again?"

He smiled down at her. "Who said it was over?"

She slapped her forehead and slow-like shook her head in disbelief, then pursed her lips for him to kiss her. He did, then began again, with his hips moving in and out to arouse her. It didn't take long until she was in rhythm with him. Her body began moving with his in unison, pleasure sweeping over them. They were off again on another soaring flight to pleasure's peak.

And then at last, his balls screamed with the ejection, and it flew out into her, and she melted away.

"Oh, my," she whispered and then closed her eyes limply.

He sat up and tried to clear his head. The sun was dropping in the west in a fiery blaze. Standing up, he pulled on
his pants and looked about at her cooking. He knelt down
and shoved some wood into the hot ashes to rebuild the fire.
She sat up, found a housecoat to wrap around her nakedness,
then moved in and gave him a shove.

"I can get it going. You won't starve. I swear I won't let
you starve." On her knees beside him, she put the coffeepot
back on the grill. Then she rose, threw her arm over his
shoulder, and kissed him.

"You better?" he asked.

"Oh, God, yes. You're a miracle. Oh." She hugged her
arms and shuddered, then raised her eyes to the clear sky. "I
know you'll have to move on—someday—but I'll miss you,
big man. I really will. I hope my memory don't ever fade
about these days we had together."

"Why's that?"

"So I can remember how neat these days have been."

"You won't. I'm going down to the creek and take a bath
while you finish fixing supper. I shouldn't be too long."

She buttoned the garment up the front. "Fine. I'll call
you."

He nodded and, armed with a towel and a bar of soap, he
went to the cold stream. His holster slung over his shoulder,
he went through the head-high willows to the shore. He hung
his gun on tree limb, handy if he needed it. He stripped off his
pants. Bathing wouldn't take him long, but maybe he'd feel
fresher by doing it. Besides, he needed to figure what he should
do next. Lathering up his body, knee-deep in the stream, he
heard the drum of horses coming from town. A quick rinse
and, dripping, he had the six-gun in his fist.

Who was coming? He fought his pants on and then hurried toward the camp. He could see, from the cover of the
willows, three men talking to Wilma. They were dressed in
suits—Pinkerton men. Didn't they ever learn that when they
dressed up in suits, outlaws and fugitives could see them
coming in Wyoming before they ever landed?

"I sure don't know where you can find Butch Cassidy and the Sundance Kid," she said, using her hand to shade her eyes against the sunset. "What did they do anyway?"

"Oh, robbed a half dozen trains and several banks."

"Why, if they stole that much money they probably ain't in Wyoming. I sure wouldn't be. I'd be on Broadway."

"Broadway?" the main Pinkerton man asked.

"Ain't that in New York?"

"Yeah, it's there. What are you doing out here?"

"Been looking for two killers the past two months who murdered my neighbor."

"Where did they go?"

"We were all over Yellowstone looking for them."

"Didn't find them?"

"Nope, they're gone like smoke."

"Your man around?"

"Taking a bath."

Pinkerton nodded. "We have to go. There's a ten thousand dollar reward on each of them."

As she bent over to tend her food, she said, "I could sure use the money."

"You find where they are, you just wire Pinkerton. The telegraph knows where we're at."

The man remounted and they rode out. Slocum went back for his towel and returned. "How was your company?"

"Pinkerton men, looking for Cassidy and Sundance. Got the reward up to ten thousand apiece. Hell, for that much, some Mormon would turn them in for it." She laughed and shook her head. "Guess they wondered why I was in a housecoat."

"How is that?"

"They kept looking at me."

Slocum laughed. "I told you that you looked much better since you straightened up your hair and took off a few pounds. They were busy calculating what was under that dress."

She narrowed his eyes. "They were staring at my body?"

"Yes. You have a nice figure these days to go with the rest of you."

She gave him a pained look. "You aren't just blowing me up?"

"No, ma'am."

"Well, I sure didn't do much to get that way."

"Wilma, you ain't half as tough as you think you are. You can't hide a nice figure, and those detectives didn't miss it."

"Come eat. This food may not be too good recooked."

"It'll be all right. I want you to dress and look nice tomorrow. We're going to find Houston."

She made a sour face. "You pushing me off on that guy?"

"No. But he has money. He doesn't have to rut around for his living or means."

"Now, why would I want to be his slave?"

"He ain't looking for a slave."

"He won't never marry me."

"You want to get married?"

"Not to him."

"Then consider becoming his housekeeper. You could do lots worse."

"I'll think on it."

He put on his shirt. The night would be cooling off soon as the sun went down. They would be in Houston's camp by the next day. He wanted Wilma to be ready to consider a job from the remittance man. He felt sure Houston was going to ask her to become his housekeeper. He'd hinted some about it—enough so that Slocum imagined the question would be presented.

He wanted to be in San Antonio when the snow fell on the Bighorns in the next six weeks. There were plenty of brown-skinned girls down there who danced and paraded their assets around the square across from the Alamo. They came in neat packages. All of them were easy to love and loved for someone to buy them drinks and watch their skills. Like minks in bed would best describe them. A winter spent like that would be more fun than stumbling through the deep snow in Wyoming. He could buy and sell enough cattle imported from below the border to finance his life of leisure down there.

The sun was down and the night insects chirped the evening away. Bats dove after insects. A coyote yapped and another answered. Wilma brought blankets for them to sit on and spread another over her shoulders while Slocum sat beside her.

"Where will you go," she asked, "when you leave me?"

"Probably San Antonio. It's warm down there in the winter months."

"You have a place down there?"

"No, I'll rent a room, buy some cattle in old Mexico, sell them up there to cover my expenses."

"Sounds pretty leisurely. You like it down there?"

He nodded. No need to tell her that, besides the warm weather, the lovely females were the biggest draw.

"Guess we better take Jennifer's horse back too when we get to my place. Her old man will soon be coming up to bring her supplies and round up the yearlings he brought her last spring. He'll be disappointed with her dead. She told me he was usually horny by the time he got there. This year he'll go home horny."

Slocum said, "He really will be." He could recall making love to Jennifer in the bunk bed. That wasn't her first time having sex with a stranger, despite her disclaimer. But with a thirty-year-old healthy woman left all alone on a mountain for long stretches, one could expect such results.

After another rousing session under the covers, Slocum and Wilma slept hard and got up before sunup. He saddled and packed. She made coffee and oatmeal. They ate the hot cereal before the sun's first purple glow slipped over the Bighorns. Then, still stiff from sleeping on the ground, they climbed into their saddles and he took the lead up the canyon. She led the packhorse.

The towering cliffs rose straight up from beside the stream. He set Red onto the narrow trail, knowing his boot would be scuffing on the wall from time to time. He hoped they'd be on top by midday and have this narrow staircase behind them.

Soon the sun rose high enough to heat up the air, and he removed his hat long enough to wipe his sweaty forehead on his sleeve. Looking forward, he rode on, talking softly to Red on the worst parts. At a wide enough spot, he reined up and offered to help Wilma down.

Both relieved their bladders and then remounted. He couldn't think of much to say except, "Onward and upward."

"Yeah," she managed in a subdued voice.

He turned back and she looked fine. He gave her a smile and wink. By noon, they had safely reached the country where the wide saddle for the pass was a grassy meadow surrounded by pines. He dropped out of the saddle and hitched up his pants, then started over to help her.

"I'm fine," she said, sounding confident, and dismounted by herself. "Damned if I don't think I'm getting tougher at this game."

He hugged and kissed her. "You're a survivor."

"Good. That was the best trip so far, up or down."

"Let's go find Houston."

"After I brush my hair. Do you think I'd look better in a dress or like I am?"

Good, she was thinking about making a good impression. "I'd save it for when we get there. Part of why I think he wants you for a housekeeper is you aren't afraid of the ways of this country."

"Me, a housekeeper?" She shook her head. "I'll have to watch my tongue, and I guess I can sweep out a tent easy enough."

Slocum laughed and they walked a good distance, leading the horses to get the kinks out of their tight muscles. In the saddle again, they soon found Houston's tent, but he wasn't in camp. Slocum went to busting up cooking wood and Wilma peeled some apples they'd found growing on a tree beside the road down at Ten Sleep.

"You know the choke cherries are about ripe down there?" she asked him.

"I'd noticed."

"There's some on the east side of the Bighorns. I may go pick some over there."

He laughed. "I thought you were over worrying about that trail."

"Lord, no, I just made it back up here is all. That was enough for a while."

Houston returned with his scoped rifle, almost out of breath. "How are you two? Did you get them?"

Slocum shook his head. "No telling where they went. We tracked them way up into the Yellowstone wilderness and finally ran out of supplies."

"Worse than that," she began. "They kidnapped a white woman, killed her husband and baby, and were dragging her around with them."

"That is simply terrible." Houston dropped into a canvas folding chair.

"Only so much you can do," Slocum said over his shoulder, busy with the axe.

"Oh, I understand, but all that tracking and they still got away."

"They'll turn up, and I'll eventually get them—if someone else doesn't lynch them before I do."

Houston agreed. "Those bloody Pinkerton agents have been burning up this trail, looking for Butch Cassidy and the Sundance Kid."

"They were in our camp down there last night asking about them," Wilma said, looking up from her cooking.

"Well, missus. How are you?"

"You can call me Wilma. All my husbands are dead and I don't want them to come back and haunt me."

Houston laughed. "Ah, Wilma, it is good to see you unscathed from all those mountains you crossed. You look very nice."

"Oh, I'm sure a couple hundred miles in the saddle did that."

"You do look very healthy. It must have agreed with you."

"I'm fine. Have you found that big ram yet?"

Slocum hadn't paid much attention, but she'd switched her clothes and was wearing the housecoat that had made the Pinkerton agents gawk at her. Good girl. She did look extra shapely in it, and Houston hadn't missed seeing that as well. Anyway, so much for that. He hoped the man loosened up enough to ask her to become his housekeeper—and maybe even his housewife, eventually.

Things went well. Her apple dumplings were a big hit as a desert to crown the rest of her food. She was busy gathering dishes and Houston was helping. Slocum went off to leave them alone to talk. Houston was asking her about Yellowstone and they were sharing stories.

It was past midnight when she slipped into Slocum's bedroll.

He woke up sleepyheaded, realizing she was naked, and she kissed him. "Aren't you going to ask?"

"Did he hire you?"

"He asked me to come work for him. Said he wasn't looking for a slave. That he'd help me like he did tonight. He'd pay me thirty dollars a month and supply me with a new tent for myself while we lived in the wilds, as he called it. Said he planned to settle down someday and we'd live in a real house in Buffalo or Sheridan."

"What did you tell him?"

"I'd let him know my decision in the morning." Her hand had found his half-full pecker and was gently pulling on it. "He can wait that long. I told him I'd need to borrow his mule to haul my few possessions over here if I decided to take the job."

He rolled over and eased himself on top of her. Kissing her and sipping on her left breast, he finally came up for air. "Good for you."

"I hope so."

He rose up enough for her to spread her legs apart, and he slipped his dick inside her. Whew, he'd damn sure miss her body. But he didn't dare winter up there in the Bighorns. Word would get out and his past—in the form of some bounty hunter—would come to find him. He needed to move on. Besides, he shivered at the thought of winter up here. Even in a bed under thick covers with Wilma tucked close for body heat, he'd get goose bumps.

Ah, she sure was like silk to ride.

14

They parted at Wilma's place after spending a day and long night together there while the north wind slapped heavy rain on her shack. The dawn brought clearing skies, and he was ready to take Jennifer's horse back to her place. He and Wilma kissed for a long time in the doorway. It was hard to separate from her, but there would be small talk in a bar somewhere in Montana or Wyoming, and his name would come up. *"Oh, he's down in the Bighorns."*

That would send some bounty hunter or hired gun in his direction. No, he'd been in the region long enough. He'd also thought lots about the letter he'd leave this time for Jennifer's husband. Bad deal, those killers getting away from him. Nothing he could have done for the poor woman they held hostage. He turned in the saddle and waved to Wilma. She was back there crying—nothing he could do about it. At least she had Houston to look after her, or her to look after him.

He settled into the saddle and, leading the packhorse, headed for Jennifer's place. Before he rode into to the yard, he surveyed the place from afar. Seeing no activity, he rode on down and turned the horse loose. With Red hitched, he went inside the house and added more to the back of the calendar on which he'd written his first note.

I am sorry to report that the above-mentioned killers of your wife escaped me in the Yellowstone Park and I lost them. They need to be brought to justice. Thanks for the use of your horse. You might check with Wilma over by Ten Sleep. She can tell you more. J.S.

He left the small ranch and moved on, knowing he wouldn't reach Buffalo before dark, but he felt he needed to escape any more reminders of his grief and concern about his failure over Jennifer. Late that night he arrived in Buffalo, left his horse at the livery, and found a room in the brick hotel. He had a late supper in the hotel restaurant and went upstairs to bed.

In the morning, he took breakfast in a diner after checking out of the hotel. At the stables, he asked the liveryman to appraise Red. At this point, he wanted to take the afternoon stage to Cheyenne. The sooner he shook this country off his coattails, the better he would feel—or at least, he hoped that new country might clear his head.

"I'd give you fifty dollars for him." The liveryman straightened from checking Red's front legs for splints.

"He's worth more than that."

"I agree, but I have to make some money too."

Slocum agreed. "I'll take it. He's a sound pony. You've got a bargain. I'm taking my saddle and gear to the stage office. I'll be back with him shortly"

The man shook his hand. "Fine. I'll be here and pay you then."

The stage depot was run by a man under a celluloid visor, who looked up from the counter when Slocum came inside the empty office and put his rig on the floor. "How far you going, mister?"

"Cheyenne."

"Fare one way is thirty dollars."

"That's fine. I'll be right back. When does it leave?"

"At two-thirty this afternoon."

"I'll be back. Hold me a seat." Slocum waved to him and walked back up the street, leading Red. He collected the money for the horse, thanked the man, clapped Red on the neck, and turned his back on the good horse, much as he had the day before with Wilma. Both separations cut deep, but they were simply an everyday reality in his life.

Saddle and bedroll loaded in the boot on the back of the stage, he took a front seat facing back and nodded to the two sleepy drummers seated in the one opposite. A nice-looking woman in her twenties showed up. She wore an expensive black velvet dress and a wide hat with balls on the fringe of the brim, and the station clerk and bowlegged stage driver started falling all over themselves to get her on board. She gave Slocum a poised smile at her entry and then took the seat beside him in a rustle of her layered dress. A rich-smelling perfume soon wound up his nose.

They left Buffalo in a charge and crack of a whip. The coach rocked and threw them together. On the way, it swung on the leather strap suspension and rocked them some more. But soon it was one with the dusty road and smoothed out some.

"My name is Carley Adams," the woman said softly to Slocum in a smoky voice.

"Nice to meet you, ma'am. Slocum's my name."

She unpinned the distracting hat, removed it, and shook her long dark curls out as if she was glad to be free. "I don't need this hat for the duration of this trip. How far are you going?"

"Cheyenne."

"I'm going there as well. What business are you in, sir?"

"Livestock dealer."

"Where are your offices?"

"Brownwood, Texas," he lied to her.

"Oh, you live way down on the border."

He nodded. "You on business or other?"

"Well." She stretched her hands out in the long black gloves and then turned to look at him. "I'm coming from my husband's funeral in Billings."

"Oh, so sorry. I apologize for asking."

She didn't look at him, merely shook her head as if to dismiss his concern. "He was hung."

Hung?

"It is very long story and maybe I should take some time to explain the entire matter."

"If you choose, ma'am." He tried to act attentive, wanting to hear her story.

"Why don't you call me Carley?"

"Whatever you like to be called." He noticed two streaking antelope race off across the rolling grassland. To the west was the outstanding range of the Bighorns. He turned back and met her gaze.

"Bernard Adams, my late husband, was a banker when I married him in Nebraska. A very sincere banker. He owned a large two-story house and had lost his first wife only a year earlier. We were happily married, and I thought we would live out our lives together. We belonged to the Methodist church, he was a lodge member. Seldom drank, never gambled, and at least as far as I know never frequented"—she lowered her voice to a whisper—"any house of ill repute, though he was very depressed over losing his first wife when I met him."

"It sounds like you were the perfect couple."

"Oh, we were. My parents had been killed in a train wreck, and I was working in a millinery when we met. The childhood sweetheart I had planned to marry since my teens had been struck dead by lightning. I really had not met another man I liked until one day Bernard came by the shop and asked me to go to church with him. That shows how thoughtful a man he was." She looked at Slocum with round brown eyes silently asking him what he thought.

"Oh, yes, sounds very sincere to me."

She raised her head up showing some pride, and he decided she possessed a beautiful neck. My, she was a great-looking woman. She had a pert bustline, and the rest of her under all the dress material looked totally inviting.

"To his shock, Bernard learned that his boss, Tom McInrow, was embezzling money from the bank. Since Bernard only owned a third of the bank, he could hardly fire McInrow. But he went to the bank board members and told them what his boss was doing. They were shocked and hardly believed him, but said they would investigate. He came home a nervous wreck that evening. I mean he didn't eat, sleep, or anything." She dropped her chin and shook her head.

"It was bad. In the morning, the sheriff came to the bank and arrested Bernard, not the president, for embezzling. I got word of his arrest and hired a lawyer friend we knew from church. That was on a Friday. The judge was out of town. So my poor husband sat in jail all weekend. Nothing the lawyer could do. And when they opened the bank on Monday, they discovered that over the weekend McInrow had taken all the money he could out of the vault and run away.

"The bank board accused Bernard of setting the whole thing up, but they were having a run on the bank and none of them wanted to face the depositors. So they made Bernard the president—a job he never should have taken. Only deputy sheriffs with shotguns could control the angry customers. They had to bar them from busting inside the bank all at once, and only let them in one at a time to talk to my husband."

The stagecoach rocked like a teeter-totter and every once in a while whirled up dust that floured the passengers in the coach. Here and there a homesteader's shack dotted the prairie beside the road. They passed several freight line wagons and long teams of oxen pulling double wagons.

"I'm sorry," she said, coughing on the dust. "Just a second and I'll continue."

Her cough at last under control, she nodded. "Of course, we lost our home, and he lost his job. Now, a stain on man's record like a bank failure marks a bank official as not worthy to manage any other financial institution. So he had no job and could not get one in any Nebraska bank or anywhere.

"We hired a detective. He located McInrow in Billings. I told Bernard to have the law arrest him up there, and they would bring him back for trial so he could clear his name. But no, the law had no money to go get such suspects. They wanted us to foot the bill for a man to go up there and bring him back. Can you imagine what that would have cost?"

"Several hundred dollars."

"Yes. I kept telling Bernard to go talk to the U.S. marshal and see what he would do. He finally did that, filled out the reports and everything. They said it would take some time, but they'd get him.

"We were living off our savings in a small apartment. Bernard grew more anxious by the day. He was a completely different person than the man I'd married. Then one day when I was out shopping he left a note that he had gone to Montana himself to arrest McInrow. I was totally shaken. He had no experience in such work.

"Six weeks later, Bernard sent me letter from the Yellowstone County Jail." She made a wry head shake and drew in a deep breath that made her breasts rise under the layers of material. "He had found McInrow and they had gotten in a gunfight. In the shooting, a woman of the night was shot and had died, and so had McInrow, who lived a short while to give a statement to an official that my husband was jealous of his affair with the dove and came in shooting.

"I, of course, rushed to Billings, but no one would listen to me. They were convinced that Bernard had come up there to kill an innocent man over a woman. So they sentenced him to death and they hung him for murder."

"What a sad story. What will you do now he's gone?"

"Find me a house in Cheyenne and live out my life, I hope."

"Good, you still must have savings."

"Yes, he provided for me. But I would much rather have had him here with me."

"I agree. But that is a sad story. You had to arrange for his burial and all?"

"Oh, yes. Now tell me your story. You have a family in Brownwood? Wife? Children?"

"No. I came out of the war and never really took root anywhere."

"There are several men like you who I have met over the years. They didn't know what to do when the war was over. It is a shame, and this country's loss."

"Not so bad. If I had settled down, I'd never have met you."

She perked up. "Yes, that is nice. You know, we're a long ways from Cheyenne. Is there a place to take a break, say, and get a room for one night's sleep, then continue on?"

"I'm certain we can, probably in Casper."

"Would you mind helping me do that? The trip down from Billings exhausted me so much I stopped and slept there last night."

What a shame. They had both slept alone the night before in the same hotel. He intended to do better than that in Casper.

The two drummers had been asleep since they'd pulled out of Buffalo. The older one woke up, took a snoot full from a pint in a paper bag, capped it, put it back inside his coat pocket, and went back to snoring.

Slocum and Carley chuckled quietly. Satisfied the drummers were asleep again, she looked up at Slocum and pursed her lips. He kissed her and then winked as he snuggled down in the seat beside her. They wouldn't need two hotel room keys in Casper. But it would be late in the night before they reached their destination.

The driver made stops at stations, took on mail, left some canvas bags, and with fresh horses quickly made off again, his whip cracking the air. The weather was pleasant, but the food available at the stage stops was poor. The outhouses were so bad, Slocum had to hold his breath and use them quickly.

Some places the steep grades slowed them to a walk. One or two places, Slocum wondered if the driver might have them unload the coach and make them walk a ways just so they could get over the top. But that likelihood partially rested with the horses' condition. Some teams were fresher than others. No doubt some had been grained more too. Long past midnight, they exchanged their stage tickets and went to the King Hotel in Casper as Mr. and Mrs. Combs. They left his saddle, pads, and war bag with the night clerk, and Slocum carried only Carley's small valise up to the second-story room.

The room was stuffy, so he opened the window a few inches. The night had cooled down, and he didn't want them to freeze in bed later.

She stood in front of the mirror, which hung over the dresser, and looked at herself glowing in the yellow-orange light of the lamp. "I guess I am still in one piece."

Then she turned and rested her bottom on the low dresser. "I must say, I am giddy as a young girl, sir. The only man in my life was Bernard. He was, of course, the only man I ever shared a bed with, or my body for that matter."

"I won't hurt you. Do you want to sleep in your clothes?"

She bit her lip and took a long time to answer. "No. I'm a grown woman. I feel I have been very brazen with you, sir. You are a very handsome man with, I guessed, an even temper. I have not had a husband—lover—in over three months. Quite honestly, I am on pins and needles because of that. Now that I have poured my heart out, help me undress. This dress is heavy and awkward, but together we can shed it."

"Do you want the light out?" he asked as she undid the many small buttons down the front.

"I don't think so. I'm trying to steel myself to this entire thing. I hope it relaxes me. I am about shaking right now."

He held the dress until she could finally step out of it. There was a hanger on the wall, and he put the dress on it, and then hung it on the nail. When he turned, she stood in her camisole and slip.

"Are you going to undress?" she asked softly.

"Yes, I am." He toed off his boots, took off his gun belt, and hung it on the ladder-back wooden chair. Then he set his hat upside down on the dresser. His vest came off, and he began to unbutton his shirt. She turned her back to him and took her camisole off. When she turned back, he saw the sway of her pear-shaped breasts, exposed with their dark, pointed nipples that made saliva flood his mouth. When his shirt was gone, he undid his pants and shed them.

She gave a small inhale. He looked up at her with a frown, then smiled. "That's part of me."

With an acceptance nod at his words, she wiggled the slip off, put it aside, and then sat on the bed to unbutton her high-top shoes with a small tool. "I should have done this first. Sorry I am so slow."

He got a good view of her shapely legs and tousled her hair playfully. Then another good look at her breasts when she looked up and pulled off the first shoe.

"You're a patient man, Slocum. My husband couldn't wait for me to do all this on our honeymoon. I still had my shoes on the first time." Her face reddened and she shook her head. "I guess I wasn't supposed to tell that. It was a wreck. But things improved after that—I don't know about tonight—"

"Don't worry."

With her shoes and stockings off at last, she dropped her naked bottom onto the bed and he joined her. With her face turned up toward his, he began to kiss her mouth, and they soon sprawled on the bed facing each other. He tasted her right nipple, and he could feel her shaking under his palm where he was holding her arm. She was real and this was going to be a big adventure. No rush, he had till morning.

Her long dark lashes squeezed shut, and she returned his kissing, pressing her flesh against him, and his world began to spin. He ran his finger up her seam, and she spread her legs apart. Then he worked on her clit and she grew more ex-cited, kissing him harder. Her hand hesitated, then she grasped his shaft. The feel of her long fingers around it made him more excited.

Her breath raced in and out; her mouth was open and she was moaning softly as he worked faster and faster on her. She motioned for him to move on top of her. He did and reached under his belly to guide his long, hard erection in her vagina. The way was already wet. She stiffened as the first inches of his cock penetrated her, but the elasticity of her cunt spread more, and he poked himself in her more and more easily until he reached her ring of fire. The opening was half the size of his dick, and he could feel the ring holding him back. But their body fluids inside were slicking up the both of them.

He pushed gently, and finally with some butt power, his dick went through her resistance and she gasped. "Oh, my, he never went that far—"

He could feel her shaking all over as he went to work on her, actually trembling as he squeezed the half moons of her butt to probe deeper as he drove his stake to the very bottom. She fainted.

He revived her slow-like, and she shook her head in disbelief under him. "This is so good. You won't stop, will you?"

He kissed her hard and went back to pounding on her ass. What a night this was going to be. She was practically a virgin. He could hardly imagine her husband never getting any deeper than that—that poor man missed half the fun. They went on and on and finally he felt himself ready to come, and then he exploded. Her fingernails dug into his back, and she gave him a final hunch before she collapsed.

Braced above her, he whispered to tease her, "You ready for some more?"

She swept the hair from her face and half rose up, checking the dimly lit room around her. "You're serious?"

"Serious as I can be."

"I'll try to keep up, but I'm awful dizzy-headed. Whew." She lay back down, looking up at him in disbelief. "I have been missing a lot. Don't tell a soul."

"I won't. Ready?"

She snuggled under him. "Hell, yes."

They made love till the sun came up. After they slept in some more, he paid for another night's lodging and took her to breakfast in a café. She looked weary but beautiful in her flushed state.

Carley fit all those poses. He wanted a photo made of her to record it, but didn't know anyone in Casper who did such work. No matter—he wouldn't have a place to keep it anyway. But she sure needed to be captured that morning on a glass negative.

Later they lounged naked on the bed, and he absorbed all of her he could. The solid breasts that, when she moved, flowed with her like willow branches in a gentle wind. He was transfixed by her looks and body. It was heady business.

"Your husband never got that deep?" Slocum asked, looking at the copper ceiling tile.

"No, but it was exciting with him. I never faulted him, but I didn't know how deep he could have gone. Well, he wasn't very large down there either. But he was good to me and very intense when he made love to me." She put her palm on her forehead. "But when you went through that ring that first time, oh my, the bells and train whistles went off."

"You even bled some?"

She quickly nodded. "A little, but I'm fine."

"How did we meet again?" he asked, teasing her as he played with her breast.

"I got on this stagecoach in Buffalo and sat beside a big handsome man, who I could tell had powers I needed to experience. Wasn't I lucky?"

"No, the luck was all mine, honey."

"No, dear, it was you who went all the way."

They had fun playing honeymooners over and over again. Then in the night they climbed on the south-bound coach and headed for Cheyenne.

He wondered about Wilma and Houston and how they were making out. She had no doubt seduced him before they'd shared his camp for very long. It made him want to laugh, wondering how deep Houston had got in her—he hoped the man was a good lover. Wilma deserved one.

Cheyenne came too fast. They spent two more frolicking nights in a fine hotel bed, and then Slocum left her for Denver.

"Leave your address for me at a saddle maker named Gary Crane on Dray Street here in Cheyenne. If I get a chance to come by and the coast is clear, who knows, I may be back up here come spring. But don't wait for me. You have your own life."

"I'm going to cry when you're gone. I won't now. But I've been a woman a long time and never knew what all I had missed about this business. Now I'm spoiled. Anything less in a partner would disappoint me."

"Don't cry for me."

She snuggled against him. "Oh, yes, I will, and when it is over, maybe I can find another lover nearly as good."

"Try hard. I'm a sugar foot."

"Yes, you are. Damn you anyhow." She feinted driving a fist into his muscle-corded belly.

Hours later he rode out under the stars, feeling empty, and never turned to look back.

15

There was knock on the door of his hotel room. Slocum reached for his .44 out of habit. "Who's there?"

"Marty Sobell. I've got a fresh-off-the-press San Antonio newspaper that you need to read, I think."

Slocum pulled on his pants, stuck the pistol in his waistband, and answered the door. He let the short man into the room and looked at the headlines on the paper the man handed him. A U.S. Army unit assigned to guard the Yellowstone Park had arrested two maniac killers inside the park's boundary. According to Captain Hightower, his men had been chasing these two killers for months. The outlaws were holding the twenty-year-old wife of a murdered homesteader as a hostage. It was alleged that the two had killed her husband and baby. Wyoming authorities said the pair had been marauding isolated landowners and Indian women. The pair—known only by their last names, Deushay and Roberson—were being held in the park jail until the spring thaw. Authorities said record snow in the park was hampering movements up there.

"They finally got them," Slocum said, nodding in satisfaction. "That poor woman probably had no mind left. What a shame."

"I figured you'd want to see that. Are you going down on the border to check on those Mexican cattle you want to buy?"

"In the morning," Slocum said, still in a daze over the news of Deushay and Roberson's capture. That would even the score for Jennifer. "I'll get dressed and be down in the plaza in a little while. I appreciate that news."

"I might tag along to the border, if you don't mind?"

Sobell was another drover he had known for years who took herds each year to Kansas. They both, he and Sobell, wanted to find an easier line of work and had talked about it extensively. "No, I don't mind. Come on. The more company the better."

Slocum dressed and went down to the tables under the bare-limbed mesquite trees. Sobell, a shorter man with a mustache, was seated in the sunshine. A bartender took Slocum's order for food, and he cradled the large cup of coffee the man brought him.

"Well, another nice warm February day in Texas," Sobell said.

"Yes, wonderful." Slocum was still in shock. The deep snow must have driven those killers out in the open, but they were finally in jail awaiting trial. And Carley was in Cheyenne, a long ways from the ruins of the Alamo across the plaza from where Slocum sat feasting on his scrambled eggs, ground pork, and chili peppers all wrapped in a flour tortilla and covered with *verde* sauce.

"Those bandits held up a train in Montana and got off with eighty thousand dollars. The ones you said you met— Butch Cassidy and the Sundance Kid," Sobell said. "They left all the gold coins. Too hard to transport, someone said. Why, I could have lived out my life on one basket of them."

"Fussy, aren't they?"

"Yeah, what were they like?"

"Kinda tough. One was as outgoing as a salesman. The other had dark hooded eyes like he suspected everyone he ran into."

Sobell lifted his cup. "They just run around loose up there?"

"It wasn't in town. They were riding the outlaw trail then, and that's way back in the Bighorn Mountains."

"Speaking of that, there were two guys that supposedly robbed their Texas boss last summer after he sold a herd in Montana."

"I met them one night too. Ward and Smith were the names they gave me. They wanted to join Butch and Sundance when I first met them. I don't think the law ever got them either."

"No, I ain't heard about that. I vaguely knew that guy they killed. Had a ranch out in the hill country. If they robbed and killed him and got all that money, they'd have enough money to lie back and keep their heads down for a long time."

"I'd guess so." Though he'd parted from her months ago, Slocum couldn't get the picture of a naked Carley out of his mind. There were plenty of dark-eyed girls shaking their butts around the plaza, and he'd sampled his share, but none of them matched being in bed with her. Whew.

"The trouble, Sobell, is they will piss away the money like those other two have, and then they'll have to make another big haul to keep up their standard of living."

The man agreed. "I'll meet you at the livery at sunup?"

Slocum nodded.

The next two days, they rode down to San Jose, a sleepy border town across the Rio Grande. The river was shallow and they forded it on horseback. Then they put up their horses and got rooms in the Inn of San Raphael. Slocum's contact there, a man named Sanchez, was supposed to meet him at the inn on the fifteenth of the month. Slocum and Sobell arrived on the fourteenth, so they relaxed in the bar and waited.

Slocum had no urge to get drunk, so he sipped some wine and talked to some of the girls who worked the bar. There was one who came in and caught his eye, and on his invitation she came over. Her name was Silvia, and she looked fully packed in a tight-fitting short leather skirt and fringed blouse that exposed enough of her cleavage to intrigue a horny male. Slocum decided he was such a person.

He ordered lunch and by then Sobell had found a woman that matched his partner. A shorter, dark-eyed witch that looked interesting enough to eat. Oh well—to eat with anyway.

After lunch, siesta was mentioned, and the two pairs parted. With her high heels clicking on the tile floor, Silvia marched with Slocum up to his room on the second floor. His two French doors were open to a balcony, and he went over to look at the street below. A warm breeze blew in and fluttered the drapes as Silvia slipped under his arm and stuck her hard breast against his chest. He noticed two gringos hitch their horses and look around. Peering over at the top of their heads, Slocum thought they looked familiar—or he'd seen them before.

"You know those two?" she asked in a smoky voice.

"I don't recognize them."

"Their names are Ward and Smith. They say there is big bounty on them in the States."

"What do they do here?"

"They bought a ranch near here."

"They amigos?"

She pulled his face down to meet hers. "No, all think they are lovers." Her head shake told him the rest.

How had they slipped down here and openly bought a ranch? Must have been lots of money in their ex-boss's pockets for them to be able to do that, or maybe they'd joined a gang and made more money that way. He'd try to avoid them.

Silvia's hand gently cupped his privates and came up with a big smile. "Ah, this will be an interesting afternoon."

Slocum turned back to Silvia. He lifted the fringed blouse off over her head and gazed at her pointed brown breasts. Perky enough looking. He dropped the garment on the bed and turned to hug her. She was packed hard as a blasting stick, and his tongue lashed with hers.

They soon were on top of the bed, coupled and going hard toward the relief at the end of the act. He closed his eyes to savor her tight pussy. Her body was a wave of muscles inside and out. And she knew how to excite a man with her various moves beneath him. But she also was worked up enough to amuse him—she wanted to be the fucker, but there was no way for her to gain that, though he enjoyed her tries. When he came at last inside of her, she bit his shoulder.

She rose up, shook her head, loosening her pinned up hair, and then flopped over on the bed as if done in. Her small shapely ass was toward him. He moved behind her. Her hand went to defend her rectum, but he held it aside and reentered her pussy quite easily. She strained some as he went deep.

"You are ready again. So soon?" she asked, sounding confused.

"Oh, darling, we ain't halfway there yet." He began to pour his meat into her. She scrambled over on her belly, and he gave her lots of pounding. When he came this time, he used the fluids to lubricate her ass.

"Oh, no," she protested, but he knew she had no say-so about what he did to her next. On her stomach underneath him, all she could do was take it—besides, he figured that when he got through with her, she might well have enjoyed all of it. His entry was slow, and she caught her scream as he pushed in, and then she beat the mattress with the sides of her fists. But soon she was away in la-la land and raised her butt in the air for him to go deeper. He came at last and they slept coupled together.

Someone knocked softly on his door an hour later.

"Yes?"

Sobell whispered, "You have company downstairs. Ward and Smith. Thought you might want to know. They don't know me."

"*Gracias.*"

"I knew you'd want to know."

Slocum walked across the room and, standing back from the window, looked out at the plaza. Silvia brought a wet cloth and gave his privates a brisk cleanup with it.

"What are you doing?" he asked, amused.

"I am going to make you stand on your toes." She tossed the cloth at the bowl on the dresser and dropped to her knees. He looked down at her shapely brown form kneeling before him, and she took his half-hard cock and sucked on the end of it.

He said no more.

That evening Slocum was approached by Ward and Smith in the bar.

"Don't we know you?" Ward asked. "You weren't all dressed up in that shack when it rained so damn hard that night in Wyoming."

"That was a real storm, wasn't it? I'm surprised to see you two down here. I saw that the gang you were looking to join had held up another express shipment."

"Yeah, well, we decided we could stay down here and not get our heads blown off," Smith said. "What brings you to Mexico?"

"Same thing brought me to Wyoming. Pussy."

Smith slapped his knee and laughed aloud. "Now, ain't that something. A man who travels all over the damn world and looks for that."

"It's safer than bank robbing."

"You ever see them two killers again, the ones you were going after?" Ward asked.

Slocum shook his head.

"Well, happy pussy hunting," Smith said, still laughing, as Slocum went over to join Sobell.

He didn't like them any better than the last time. Anyone that would shoot his boss in the back, bury him God knew where, and take his money was liable to do anything. They'd nimbly made it to Mexico and were going to live the good life as long as their money lasted.

"Reckon the law knows they're down here?" Sobell asked.

"The law has no money to go after them north of the border, let alone in Mexico where there is no law."

"What are they worth?" Sobell asked quietly, as if considering something about them.

"I think a thousand that the family had offered at the outset."

"That real?"

"Damned if I know. Lots of big rewards never get paid."

"Who offered that reward?"

"Told you—family, I think. I guess we can check with a wire to the county sheriff up at Mason County."

Sobell nodded, looking deep in thought. "I'll do that later this afternoon."

"You needing money?"

"Be a shame not to take it." The man smiled at the notion. "Why wouldn't we do that? And not have to deal with men like Sanchez, buying cattle that he probably stole."

"If the money is in a bank, it looks like it might be like you say—easy."

Sobell shook his head. "I don't care if they'll come easy or come feetfirst. Pays the same."

"They might be tougher than you think."

Sobell ordered another drink and ignored his warning. "When's Sanchez coming?"

Slocum chuckled. "This is Mexico. Maybe today." He turned his palms up.

"Maybe. Yeah, we are south of the border. Time means nothing down here. Where's Silvia?"

"Said she had business to take care of."

"Business, huh?"

"I'm not sure. She's real enough. Maybe too real."

"Too real?"

"She ain't there to simply turn tricks for a few bucks. There's more to her than that. She never charged me. I don't know what else she is, but she's a schemer."

Sobell grinned. "Funny how you can tell something is up with one of them, no matter how hard they fuck you."

"There's got to be schemers in this world."

Before they went to supper at a small café that Sobell's woman said made wonderful dishes, Sobell sent his telegraph from the federal telegraph office. Then the two women met them at the candlelit table and they had a great meal of tender beef, spicy enchiladas, sliced avocadoes, and fried apple pie. They washed the meal down with red wine, then leisurely walked the two blocks of dark street back to the hotel.

Sanchez had not checked in to the hotel yet. The cattle buyer would come sooner or later, so Slocum excused himself and Silvia, and the two of them started up to his room, Slocum following her up the stairs. She wore a tight blue silk dress and high heels that showed lots of her tan legs to very good effect. Not an outfit anyone would show up to attend church in, but the garment fit her shapely body and made things interesting to look at.

He unlocked the door and let her go in ahead of him, then struck a match and lifted the globe enough to see her undoing the front of her dress. Saliva flooded his mouth as the image of her naked body filled his mind.

He toed off his boots and then he prepared to help her out of the dress. Soon her flesh spilled out of the half-shell opening, and her tawny body emerged. The dark nipples looked like they were pointed at him. With his suspenders down, his pants fell, and he stepped out of them and walked to her. He gathered her into his arms and kissed her mouth, finding her hot tongue in his mouth. In his arms, she squirmed until it felt like her muscled body was a huge snake's. His fingers combed through her soft pubic hair, and she moved her legs apart for his finger to probe the crease. The lips of her cunt were already wet with her juices and he smiled, rekissing her. Her nail-like pointed nipples stuck to his bare chest. He savored her closeness and the previews of what was ahead for him to enjoy.

They were on the bed, making the ropes squeak in protest under them. His rock hardness made his entire dick feel ready to blow up, the powerful muscles inside of her crushing his efforts to plunge in her any more than halfway. Not to be denied, the muscles in his butt began to win the depth battle. She strained hard, but his power took over and he was slamming his dick against the bottom of her vagina. By the moaning deep in her throat and the wild look of her hair in her face as she shook her head from side to side, he knew he had won the second battle. He plunged to the bottom and exploded.

From there on she was his to do with as he wanted—but he did it gently. They finally collapsed to sleep in each other's arms.

He opened his eyes, his foggy vision making out the sunlight spilling in through the two French doors. Looking over beside him, he saw that Silvia's tawny bare body was in a fetal position on her side. A pretty woman sleeping. He dressed and smiled at her soft breathing.

He bent over and kissed her cheek. Then he left the room and found Sobell in the restaurant. The waiter brought Slocum a steaming cup of rich coffee. With a nod to Sobell, he took the yellow telegram the man handed him.

"The thousand dollar reward is in the Texas National Bank. Family will pay," said Sobell.

Slocum raised his gaze up from the telegram to look at the man. "Where do they pay at?"

His partner shrugged. "I imagine Texas."

"They killed their boss in either Montana or Wyoming. They'll have to be tried up there."

"I say take them to Mason, Texas, collect the reward, and that should be enough. Fifty-fifty."

Slocum shook his head in deep doubt. "It may not be that damn easy."

"Hell, Slocum, what can they do but pay us if we bring them two killers?"

"I hope they will."

"Let's do some figuring how we're going to do this. They don't look all that tough."

The waiter brought Slocum his plate of food, and he waited until the man was gone before he commented again. "When you face a hanging charge, you can get your back up."

"That's lots of money."

Slocum agreed, then set into eating his tortilla-wrapped breakfast. Where was that damn Sanchez at anyway?

Sleepy-eyed, Silvia came down and joined them. She leaned wearily toward Slocum. Not close enough, she scooted the chair over to cling to him and moan some. "I am so sore. Did you use sandpaper on me last night? I think I need to sit in a cool tub of water all day." Her hand slipped to her waistband and she rubbed her crotch. "I am on fire. Did you use chili powder too?"

"No. Just me," he said, a little uncomfortable with her complaining so publicly.

"I have to go to Santa Maria today. Could you rent a rig and take me? My grandmother is going to be ninety years old. She would be glad to see me."

Slocum stood up. "Get your things. I'll rent a horse and buggy. We can leave in thirty minutes." He turned to Sobell. "That damn Sanchez comes, you stall him for me. I'll be back."

"Sure, no problem. You think more about that pair. I'm damn near broke myself."

"I will. You get more particulars."

"I can do that. Don't worry. I can keep Sanchez here."

Silvia had left on the run to get "some of her things," and Slocum finished his coffee standing up, gave Sobell a head toss that he was leaving, and went to the livery. He rented a fast horse and a two-person buggy with a top on it and swung around to pick Silvia up. She had two carpet bags, so he tied off the horse and loaded them on the small rack in back.

"Will they stay on there?" she asked, sounding concerned.

He nodded, strapping them down tight, then put her on the seat. She scooted over to make room for him. From all the items she had, Slocum decided that she must make big money or had a rich godfather. They left the streets of the border town behind, and he drove where she directed, south on the busy road.

"How far away is this place?" he asked when at last she turned to him, put a hand on his shoulder, and jabbed a breast in his side to get cozy.

"Oh, not too far."

"Far?"

She kissed him on the cheek. He'd noticed she wore a long skirt and blouse and a flat-topped hat like many Spanish ranch women wore—a much milder outfit than the other two he'd seen her in.

"We are going where?"

"To see my grandmother."

"Who else?"

"My father."

"You about to get me in trouble with him?"

"No, no. I will tell him you were so nice to bring me down there to his hacienda and such a gentleman. He will like you."

"Oh, yes, and when he finds out I'm fucking his daughter, he will shoot me."

"No, but if I don't go home for Grandmama's birthday, he will cut off the money he sends me to stay up here. That is what he said in his telegram." She sat back and held her hand to her forehead like she had a headache.

"So you didn't have money to take transportation back home?"

"That would be such a boring ride. This way"—she perked up like she was excited to be with him—"I have you to entertain me."

"I don't like it. If some old cowboy brought my daughter home and he wasn't going to marry her, I'd shoot him."

She turned his head to face her. "That is an idea."

"No, it ain't, and I am not being used to make a lie."

She rose up and kissed him on the mouth. "I never charged you, did I?"

"I never paid you."

"Good, then you owe me much money."

"How much?"

"Oh, lots of money for all you did to me in the bed. I am still sore. No, I'm not a *puta*. But I do like to make love and my father knows that, so he sends me money to enjoy myself up here on the border, and I don't embarrass him in the village near his hacienda."

Slocum took a breath and looked at some longhorns with calves busy grazing in the mesquite and grass that covered the rolling hills. The calves were roan crosses. In a few years, all the cattle in the southwest would be of some British breed. Shorthorn was a popular cross.

He was still in a quandary about this trip she hauled him away on—to see her grandmama. Then, it was her father who kept her up in San Jose. He must have a big hacienda to afford her. How much did he know about his daughter's wild ways, which he was financing?

He slapped the horse with the lines to speed up his gait. How far away was the hacienda anyway? As time went on he grew a little more impatient with her evasive answers.

"How much farther is this place?" he asked.

She looked hurt. "Still a ways."

"How far do we have to go?"

"I'm sorry. It is still a ways."

No matter, he couldn't get too mad at her. They were on the road, and he might as well accept it.

By late afternoon, they stopped in a small dusty town and took a room in the hotel as Mr. and Mrs. Crown. The clerk promised the couple there were no bugs in their rooms. They ate supper in the hotel dining room, and she drew lots of looks from men in the room. Even in everyday clothes, she was an eyeful, and she knew it.

While eating across from her, in a soft voice he asked her, "Have you ever been married?"

She wrinkled her nose at him. "It was very bad. He was a jerk. He got drunk and passed out the night of our wedding. I was a virgin then. The next night he went out to some whorehouse, left me in the room, came in after midnight stinking of cheap perfume, and said he was going to consummate our marriage. He was too drunk to get it up, and I went home the next morning without him."

"That was a heartbreaker."

Her dark eyes narrowed to slits. "I was so mad, I could have killed him if I had had a gun. Of course, my father had the marriage annulled. Do you know how that went over in a small village?" Her eyes like cold steel bored into him. She shook her head from side to side. "That goofy rich girl is so cold in bed, she can't keep a husband. I didn't want a husband."

He reached over and patted her hand. "That was tough. I'm sorry I even asked."

"Then, like a fool, I fell in love with a married man. I was going to show everyone. He was good in bed too. I was dumb. My father learned about our affair. He and I talked one whole night. He said that I must shut this man off. I told him no, that I needed him, I was addicted to him. He said no, you're addicted to men, like your mother was. Then we reached a compromise. I was to move to San Jose, where he would support me."

"Did your mother leave your father?"

"Yes. I never knew her. I grew up in the casa and had everything I wanted. Someday, he wants me to find a real man and return to run the hacienda. Interested?"

"Would you want to be a housewife? No parties, no drinking and flirting with men. Be the lady of the house and worry about meals and lazy help."

She wrinkled her nose at him. "Good as you are in bed, yes. But I can't say I wouldn't meet a man and want him for a night or even a couple of days to have a honeymoon."

"If I get shot in Mexico by an angry father, it will all be your fault."

"He won't shoot you. I promise. You may even like him." She hugged Slocum to her breast and kissed him sweetly on the cheek. "If I had had you on my wedding night, I'd have lived out my life with you. Where were you at?"

"Probably sleeping with my hand for a lover, driving cattle to Kansas."

She laughed aloud. "No wonder you are so big in bed. My, that would have been boring."

The second night they slept in hammocks in an old woman's yard and hit the road before daylight. She tried to honey up to him so he wouldn't be angry at her about the long trip. It almost worked.

On the third day, they reached the Grande Hacienda. Slocum saw palm trees, manicured flower beds, and, as the buggy's rims crunched a seam in it, a driveway that he'd guess was raked down by hand every day.

Small girls came running beside the buggy, screaming that La Donna was home. Servants came from the house to get her luggage. They bowed to Slocum when he got down, and he shook their hands instead. Then he helped Silvia down. This was not the Silvia he knew. On the ground, she looked elegant, hugged the dusty children to her skirt, and talked to all of them.

A tall, stern-faced woman in her forties came out and shooed the children away. They left reluctantly, then Silvia introduced him. "Madonna, this Slocum—I don't know if that is his first or last name, but that is what he calls himself. Slocum, Madonna is the majordomo of my father's house."

Slocum thought Silvia might have embarrassed the woman. "Come inside," Madonna said and showed them the way. "I guess they have all your luggage?"

"I think so. Slocum needs some fresh clothes, a bath drawn. We left all his things in San Jose when I realized that Grandmama was having a birthday. We were in such a hurry. But we are here."

"Tomorrow. Your father is out working stock with some vaqueros."

"Good. We both can be cleaned up and ready for supper. We will stay in the south suite."

"It will be ready for you both. Bath water in thirty minutes." She looked Slocum up and down. "I have clothes to fit him. They will also be delivered."

Silvia hugged her arm. "You are so organized, Madonna. Thanks so much."

Madonna turned to Slocum. "I was so excited to see my girl, sir, I may have forgotten my manners. Welcome to the Grande Hacienda."

"No, you were fine. Thanks so much for your hospitality."

Silvia took him through the great room and down the shadowy hallways to a thick door with the image of a fire-breathing dragon carved into the wood.

"Man, that is a monster," he said, holding the door open for Silvia.

"No, that is my guard dog." She laughed freely and began to undress. "Can you believe this place?" She held her hand out toward the opulent setting of a huge, high bed, wall hangings, and French doors letting in a warm wind. There was a six-foot painting of a woman in a fine dress on one wall, perhaps a little too sexy for most formal paintings, but she was a looker.

"That is the woman I never knew," Silvia said with her arms wrapped around him.

He studied the face and finally said, "I can see you in her."

"Others say the same. I have talked to people who work here that knew her, and they said we came from the same marble."

He nodded. She finished undressing and slipped into a white robe just before a knock came at the door.

"Please let them in," she said to him.

He agreed and opened the dragon-decorated door. A half dozen men and women carried buckets of hot water and towels, and one gray-headed man brought a stack of men's clothing.

"If they don't fit you, senor, ask for more."

"Gracias," Slocum said, and set them on a vanity. "I will do that."

Satisfied, the man nodded and left ahead of the bucket brigade.

Silvia was thanking them as she herded them out and put the latch in place. Shaking her head over the matter of running them off, she turned and opened the robe for Slocum to see her naked.

"I'm a real whore, aren't I?"

He shook his head and toed off his boots. "I never paid you a dime."

"Good, I still have a chance." She set the robe aside, stepped over dainty-like, and slid down into the smaller of the high-backed copper tubs. "I saved the big one for you. I hope you fit in it."

"I'll figure it out," he said and finished undressing. The water felt hot enough to his hand, and he anticipated that the warmth would loosen his back muscles, which were tight from driving the buggy for three days to get here.

When they finished bathing and had dried off, he tossed her onto the bed as though she were a feather and climbed in to join her. She recovered from his toss and sat up with her arms out for him. "Now we can get sticky all over again."

After supper at the great table, Silvia's father, Raúl, invited Slocum into his den that contained books, bookshelves, and a great desk. Some of the books were American classics; others were Spanish books on many things, from trade to scientific books on cattle and horse diseases.

Raúl poured them each some whiskey in crystal glasses and offered Slocum a Cuban cigar. The end of the cigar cut off, her father lit the smoke for him, then did the same for himself. He pointed to the deep leather chairs, and they took their drinks and sat down. There were some very different patterns of cowhides on the floor.

"Well, senor, welcome to my casa. I must thank you for bringing my daughter back."

"My pleasure. You have a lovely daughter, a fine staff, and a great casa here."

"My casa is a source of great pride for me, and there is only one thing important to me: my daughter. Is she all right?"

"She's fine. We met a few days ago. She said she needed to come home for her grandmother's birthday. So I drove her down here, not knowing what I'd find."

Raúl nodded. "Did you worry about coming here with her?"

"Matter of fact, at first I was nervous."

Raúl nodded as if considering the words. "I am not an angry man. My wife had this same condition. Back then, I was young and vain and could not understand what she was doing. I know now I should have done things different— maybe? Maybe not? But I saw she needed to be free. I worry about men taking advantage of my Silvia."

"She is not some dumb girl. She may never find herself, but you had a price to pay to keep her. You have done well."

"Will she ever settle down?"

Slocum blew a mouthful of smoke at the bright lamps overhead. "I think she wants control of a man, like one wants a bronc horse to be broken. But she won't stay with him when he finally is like that."

Raúl nodded as though he thought the same thing. "You are a wise man, Slocum. She picked well. Now, what I can I do to repay you for bringing her home?"

"Sell me five hundred big steers that I can send to market in Kansas and make some money."

"No problem. Is that enough?"

"That would suit me fine."

"When do you want them?"

"Middle of March in San Antonio. How much will they cost?"

"Oh, fifteen dollars a head. I can send some of my men to drive them up to San Antonio for you. And you can pay me this fall."

"Oh, that might be asking too much. I can raise the money for them."

"Don't do that."

"Do you want a note?"

"We are men with an understanding. We can shake hands."

Slocum did that and then downed the whiskey. "It must be Christmas—I came here to bring Silvia home and found just what I was looking for for business. I need to go send a telegram."

"Write it out. One of my men can go to the office in the morning and send it for you."

"Gracias." Sanchez could go to hell. Slocum would have Sobell tell Sanchez he'd made a better deal.

They drank more whiskey and talked about horses and war. At last, a few hours later, Slocum went down the hall to the dragon-door room. He tried the door and found it unlocked, and when he opened the door to step inside the dimly lit room, out of nowhere a pillow hit him in the face.

Silvia stood naked as Eve in the middle of the bed. "I didn't bring you down here to talk all night with that old man."

"Well," he said, toeing off his boots, "you never said he was such a real nice guy. I couldn't just jump up and leave him."

"You are mine, not his." She came flying off the bed to attack him.

"Darling, you must have worked up a real mad while I was gone." He caught her up in his arms and then threw her back on the bed. "Hold your horses. I'm coming."

Undressed, he climbed in and pinned her down on the silk sheets.

"And another thing: Stop tossing me in bed. . . ."

He smothered her mouth with his. What a hellcat.

16

Back in San Jose, he caught up with Sobell in the plaza the morning after they arrived back. The drover was eating oatmeal, complaining about his stomach.

"About time you got back here. That damn Sanchez called you everything but a white man when I broke the news to him. You really get some cattle down there?"

He slurped more of his milky oatmeal off his spoon, and then looked up for an answer.

"I have five hundred big steers coming from Mexico that cost fifteen dollars a head, and I have them financed."

"Holy shit. You need a partner?"

"No, but I need a drover."

Sobell dropped his chin for more cereal. "I guess I can crank one up."

"The cattle will be in San Antonio in mid-March."

"Damn, when you go off, you make good deals."

Slocum looked around to be certain no one would hear him. "Now, where are we at with those two boss-killers?"

"They stay in old Mexico. Them boys ain't crossing the Río Bravo unless they got a rope around their neck and hands tied on the horn."

154

"And we can collect the reward up in the hill country?" Slocum asked.

"I ain't too sure about that. The sheriff said we could, but he ain't got the money, I'd bet. It's in the bank, and they might shake us down on the amount."

"What if I run up there, meet the family, and get their word we can collect it?"

"Wouldn't hurt none. I heard they stay close to their ranch. I don't think anyone will spook them away from there. I sure could use my part of it." Sobell looked over at him hard.

"Take me two days to get up there, a day or so to find them, and two to get back. I'll wire you to have saddle horses ready if I'm certain we can collect it."

"Good." Sobell slumped in the chair and rubbed his flat belly. "I eat that damn many hot peppers again, I want you to kick my ass. By the way, where is that slinky lady you were with?"

"I left her up in the room sleeping."

"I wouldn't leave her anywhere. Man, she is good-looking."

Slocum nodded. Later on he would tell Sobell about her, her father, and his arrangement with the man. That could wait. At the moment, he needed a horse and buggy and her up and ready to go.

He ate his tortilla-wrapped breakfast and drank down some more rich coffee before he left money for his meal, and left Sobell to his bellyache.

Silvia, a little sleepy eyed, had no desire to miss going with him. "I will wear my ranching clothes?"

"That would be better, yes."

"No problem." She was kneeling on the edge of the bed, waiting for a kiss. Her fancy lace nightgown was open down the front, and he took a good feel of her right breast while he kissed her.

She shook her head at him after he stepped back. "Oh, I'll get you—later."

In a half hour, her things were loaded and strapped down. They left in the buggy at a fast jog. Grain feeding on their last trip had really shaped up the gelding, which he called Harry, into a high condition, and he moved out smartly. The river was shallow enough to cross.

"Damn," she said when they were on the American side, shocked at the horse's pace. "He's about to race this morning."

Slocum laughed. He hoped this trip was as good as his last one. The company was sure sweet anyway.

They spent the night on the El Paso Road in a small inn. The place was clean, and since they had to be quiet or wake up the house, they managed to keep their lovemaking to a softer noise level. After the breakfast the innkeeper's wife cooked, they were headed northwest and arrived in Mason past lunchtime. After they checked into the small hotel, Slocum went to find the Whitackers and left Silvia to rest. The postal clerk told him they lived on Weldon Creek and drew a map.

"This is the family that lost a man up north in a robbery-murder?"

"Laferty Whitacker. That's him. Did they ever find his body?"

"I don't know. Thanks." Slocum took his map and left.

Over supper in a German restaurant, he told Silvia about his deal and asked if she wanted to go along in the morning.

"Sure, see some new country and be with you."

His spoiled girl was on the happy side, so he took her back to the room and made her happier.

Afterward, they lay on their backs and the streetlights below illuminated the tin squares in their ceiling.

"Did you like the hacienda?" she asked.

"What I saw of it, yes. I spent most of my time behind the dragon."

She was tickled at that and laughed till she cried. "Behind the dragon is funny."

He agreed, curled around her, and dropped off to sleep.

Whitacker's Ranch was an impressive place. Big two-story whitewashed house with corrals, windmills, and a row of old jacals for the help to live in. A blond woman in her thirties, maybe early forties, came out on the porch holding her shoulder-length hair to one side in the south wind.

He took off his hat. "Ma'am, I hate to bother you, but is this where the Whitackers live? The family that lost their man?"

"Yes, sir. Would you and your woman like to come in? I have fresh coffee made."

"Silvia, she wants to talk inside."

"I'm coming," she said and came off the buggy before he could get over to help her.

The woman, who gave her name as Nan, had them sit down at a large table. "Why are you asking about my husband?"

"The two men who are accused of the robbery can, I think, be located. But it will be dangerous and require some expenses."

She finished pouring coffee in their cups and sat down to listen.

"Now, I know the law talks a good game," Slocum told her. "But they have not caught them."

"I agree. Is that your business? Go find and catch them?"

"It is from time to time." Silvia was all ears, since she'd only heard bits and pieces of the situation before this meeting.

"Mister, there is a thousand dollars in the Texas National Bank in Mason if you can bring them two dead or alive to the jail."

"Ma'am, how will I know you will pay it?"

Nan blinked her eyes at him. "They killed my husband. They stole several thousand dollars from him that he collected from a cattle dealer in Billings. I have a receipt they sent me showing the amount, twelve or so thousand dollars, that they paid him."

"I doubt they have any of that money left. I'm sorry."

"That won't be any problem. I want to see them hang. I'll pay you or whoever a thousand dollars for capturing them."

"Now, I'm talking about delivery here. They'll have to be tried in Montana."

"Mister, if I have to drag them feetfirst up there myself, I want them hung."

Slocum sipped his coffee. Good rich Arbuckles. "Then if we do find them, we can collect the total reward."

"Damn right."

"No problem. But many times local law forces expect a large portion of the reward for themselves."

"You get them. I'll pay you the whole thing."

"Your coffee is right good. Thanks."

"You and your lady want to spend the night? You are welcome to stay here and head back in the morning. I'm pretty well alone. My sons are off working cattle and won't be in for a couple of days. They'll be glad that someone is going to try to arrest those killers. Those two worked here for us for three years. Greed, greed is a terrible thing."

Slocum agreed. The woman must have folded and unfolded her hands a thousand times before they left her the next morning. She and Silvia had some soft conversation. The woman never asked if they were married, but she said to Silvia, "I hope you never lose your man like I did. It's a sad state of affairs. We worked side by side for years, and when we finally were on top, they killed him."

In the morning, they headed back to the border, knowing they had two days of hard driving. Rain came in from the gulf by midday and slowed their return. Soggy and cold, they found some lodging at an inn. Slocum put the horse in a stall out back and fed him grain and hay he'd paid the innkeeper for. Supper was a lot less appetizing than they had had elsewhere: boiled potatoes, sauerkraut, and day-old bread. It was still raining the next morning, and they went on early, since the prospect of more sauerkraut for their breakfast held no interest for them. At the next crossroads, they feasted on hot bread, cow butter, and good coffee in a small store.

The light rain misted their faces all the way, but finally they made it back to Mexico. Sobell was inside at a table, looking at the rain-streaked window.

"How was Mason?" he asked.

"Wet. Need I say more?"

"I thought about you all day. How is your woman?"

"Wrinkled."

Sobell laughed. "What did you learn?"

"The dead man's wife will pay us the whole amount if we can deliver the men to Mason. She's about given up on the law ever capturing them."

"So we need to coax them across the Río Bravo?"

"Hell, no. We'll go put them in handcuffs and leg irons. Arrest them, chain them up, then take those two up to Mason."

"I guess there won't be no baiting them, then?"

Slocum shook his head. "We ain't messing with them."

Sobell rubbed his palms on his pants. "We go after this rain passes?"

"Fine with me. I'll go buy the handcuffs and leg irons."

Very somber, Sobell said, "I guess it'll work."

Slocum nodded. "It'll work." They'd make short work of this deal. He couldn't imagine many folks defending or aiding those killers. But one could never tell.

17

A cold north wind replaced the rain the next morning. Dressed warmly, Slocum and Sobell bought a packhorse, camping supplies, and bedrolls. Slocum sent Silvia north in a buckboard to catch a stage to San Antonio. He'd told her they'd be from five to seven days locating the killers, arresting them, and taking them up to Mason. He'd meet her in San Antonio at the Eagle Hotel. The clerk would give her a key to his room. That would be a good place to hook up with her again if it all went well.

The two killers had not been to town for several days. Slocum dismissed his partner's concern. "They'll come in. This is the closest place for them to get drinks and women."

The second night, Smith and Ward came into the cantina to drink and shoot pool.

"You guys looking for a ranch down here?" Ward asked.

Slocum nodded. "We've been looking around."

Smith leaned on his pool cue. "There're several places for sale. We looked at a large ranch south of here. But you'd need lots of money."

Sobell shook his head. "We ain't got that much."

They shot some friendly pool until Ward said they had to

160

go home. Slocum watched as Smith finished his beer. They started for the front door. Slocum and his partner went outside friendly-like to see them off. Walking behind them, he nodded to Sobell and drew his six-gun.

He stopped Ward, and Sobell took Smith. When they were disarmed, Slocum made them face the wall, feet back so they leaned with their hands on the cantina adobe wall.

"What are you two up to?" Ward growled. "You ain't Mexican law."

"You'll see." He knew that Sobell would need some time to saddle and load the horses before he got back.

The clock ticked slowly. Slocum put their handguns in the saddlebags on one of their horses. He'd get them out later; the barrels were gouging him. At last, Sobell came back, leading their horses. He hitched them at the rail and brought the handcuffs. The pair grumbled when he cuffed them, but Slocum told them to be quiet or he'd bust their heads in. They loaded each prisoner onto a horse, then chained their legs under the bellies of their horses and secured the cuffs to the horns. With leads on the killers' horses, Slocum and Sobell mounted up and left the village with the packhorse coming behind.

They crossed the Rio Grande under the stars and halted on the sandy north side. Slocum looked back at Mexico in the night, grateful to be on the U.S. side. In the starlight, he checked their prisoners' horses and their cuffs, which all looked good.

He took their six-guns out of their saddlebags and transferred them to his. Ward had lost his hat in the river crossing, and he was snarling about what he was going to do to them when he got free.

Slocum rode in close, grasped his shirt. "I said shut up. I mean that. I'll gag you or bust your head open. That wanted poster says dead or alive."

Ward stared back in defiance, but he didn't say anything more. They rode on.

An hour later, Smith began talking. "We've got money in

Mexico. We can go back there and we'll give it all to you."

"How much you got left?" Sobell said, bringing up the rear. "They'll pay a thousand dollars for the two of you."

"We've got that much."

"Shut up," Ward said. "I don't trust these bastards."

Slocum wondered how much they got from Whitacker up there. He tried to recall the amount the cattle broker told her they had paid him. Didn't make any difference; he felt the same way that blond woman did: They needed to face punishment for their crimes.

Dawn broke and they were on the road north. At Sims Corner Store, a deputy sheriff stopped them and asked about their prisoners.

"They killed in Montana last summer. We're bounty hunters."

"Who are they?"

"Ward and Smith. They stole from and killed a rancher from Mason, Texas, who they worked for and who had sold a large herd up there."

The deputy nodded. "I heard about them."

"The man's widow wants to see them face the law."

"I don't blame her."

"We'll be going on."

"Thanks, they look tough. Guess even bounty hunters have a hard time with outlaws like them."

"See ya," Slocum said, and they rode on. When they stopped off the road, he unlocked the belly chains, then one cuff on one of them so he could relieve himself. Then he put that one back on his horse and did the other one while Sobell covered them with a rifle.

They chained them to a tree at night and took turns watching them. The fourth day, when Slocum unlocked the leg chains, Ward flew out of his saddle on top of Slocum. A glancing blow from the cuffs sent Slocum back on his butt. Hampered by the cuffs, Ward couldn't recover fast enough to charge him before Slocum kicked him in the head and sent him spinning across the ground.

"You can piss in your pants from here on," Slocum said and jerked him up and put him roughly in the saddle. When Ward was chained underneath and his hands were locked on the saddle horn, Slocum stepped back and caught his breath.

"Just piss in your pants," he said and mounted his horse.

"I'm sorry," Sobell said. "I should have shot him."

Slocum shook his head. "I should have figured he'd try that. I told you, facing the gallows they'd get desperate." His hand felt the left side of his face, where Ward had hit him. That place would be sore, but nothing was broken. With a deep breath, he swung into the saddle and they rode on.

When they crossed the Pedernales River, Slocum knew they'd be in Mason in less than a day. The weather was cool, and he rode under a blanket. He had not slept for more than a few hours of uncomfortable rest since they left Mexico. His partner was about to fall out of the saddle, he was so beat.

"Sobell?" No answer. Slocum reined up his horse and turned to see him slumped over his saddle. Slocum dismounted and went by the pair.

"I'm sorry. I can't go another mile." Sobell half fell off his horse, and Slocum caught him to break his fall. Holding his head up, Slocum felt lost.

"We'll sleep a few hours after I chain them to a tree."

Sobell nodded. "Good idea."

With their prisoners chained to a large cedar tree, Sobell kicked out his bedroll and thanked Slocum. His back to a large rock, Slocum sat with a rifle over his lap. They had decided small town jails might not hold their prisoners, so they'd pushed hard to get them to Mason. Making only short stops to nap along the way and then moving on, until they'd worn themselves completely out.

There was some loud shouting that woke Slocum, who jerked up his rifle, ready to shoot.

"Mr. Slocum?" A blond boy on horseback looked wide-eyed at him. "We had word you were coming."

"You Nan's son?" he asked.

"Yes, sir."

He sighed. "Glad you're here. Who else?"

"My brother Glen and Toby Hawks."

"Don't hurt them, the law can do that. Just guard them. No vigilante stuff."

"We won't."

"Me and Sobell haven't had any sleep in five days."

"Mr. Slocum?" The older boy was squatted on his heels. "I'm Glen, and Maw said to find you and be sure you get them killers to Mason."

Slocum looked at him hard. "You expecting any trouble?"

"No, sir. The word was out that you two were bringing them in, so we came looking to help you. We know them. Them's the ones killed Dad."

"Anyone else know you boys are out here?"

"I don't reckon so. Why?"

"Let us nap a little. Then we can ride on into town."

"Sure, we'll guard them while you do that."

Slocum decided he had done all he could. He laid his head down and slept awhile. His partner woke him. "We've drawn a crowd."

A quick look and he could make out about twenty men and boys, all armed, squatting around their camp. He climbed up to his feet, stiff as a man more than twice his age.

Quietly men came, shook his hand, and thanked him. No doubt the man those two had killed had had lots of friends. They helped load the prisoners onto their horses. Mounted, Slocum led the pair. Sobell brought the packhorse, and they all rode for Mason.

At every crossroads folks gathered, took off their hats for them, and waved. Word must have really spread about them coming, Slocum decided. The roads were soon full of people who came to see them and their prisoners. Buggies, wagons, horses, and some bicycles clogged the road. Slocum rode around them, and they cleared a way. He could see the courthouse a block ahead. Shotgun-armed guards stood in the street to meet them and to deter any force that wanted to take the law into their hands.

"Ever seen anything like this before?" Sobell called out to him.

"No. Kinda spooky, ain't it?"

"It is. I never dreamed we'd get this much attention."

"Maw's going to want you to come out and stay with us." Glen said.

"I bet if we can sleep for two days, we'll join her."

"Good. You two can sure do that."

A white-haired man with a badge on his suit coat came out into the street to meet them and introduced himself. "Otto Meercker. I am the sheriff of Mason County."

Slocum nodded. "You know these two will have to be transported to Montana for trial. There are warrants for their arrest up there. I don't want any slick lawyers getting them out of your jail."

He nodded. "If I have to deliver them myself, they will face justice. The man they killed was a leading citizen in our community."

"I understand."

"They will be held for the law or we will ship them up there."

That night after a bath arranged by the Whitacker boys and a fine supper their mother fixed, Slocum and Sobell fell asleep on some beds upstairs and slept till midmorning. When they came downstairs, she fixed them a sawmill breakfast of omelets, grits, fried bacon, and biscuits with gravy. Arbuckles coffee flowed, and at last they sat back and grinned.

"Fuller than a tick," Sobell said.

"Fuller than that," Slocum added.

Mrs. Whitacker—Nan—sat across the table from them and had been part of the conversation through the meal. "Did you know these men?"

"No," Sobell said. "I met them in Mexico. Slocum knew them and told me about them when we were in Mexico. I said that it should be easy. 'Let's collect the rewards.' But it wasn't easy."

"What if we go into town and get that settled tomorrow?

I know you two can sure use the rest for another day."

"We can," Slocum agreed. "Next time, I'll listen more to my own thinking. It turned out to be a real tough job."

She nodded. "What will you do now?"

Sobell smiled at her. "I've got a herd of cattle to take north shortly."

"What about you, Slocum? You taking your wife somewhere?"

He smiled at her. "We're just good friends."

She looked up at the ceiling tiles for help and smirked. "Sorry."

"Don't worry about it. Those criminals are in jail, and things are as you wanted."

Two weeks later, Slocum met the Grande Hacienda men at the Rio Grande and they drove the five hundred steers to San Antonio. Tall-framed longhorn steers, the ones that brought the highest price on the Kansas market. It was a slow drive and took a week. They used a squeeze chute to brand them on a place west of the Alamo. Sobell had leased it as a setup to gather the rest of his herd for the drive north. Slocum thanked each of the vaqueros and paid them twenty dollars apiece as a bonus for bringing them up there. They all smiled and took off their sombreros to thank him. Silvia had come out from San Antonio to join him and oversee it all.

He rode over and stepped off the cow pony they had brought from Mexico for him to ride on the drive, one of three super animals Raúl had sent as a gift to his amigo Slocum.

"Your father spoils me as much as he does you," he said, nodding to the gray horse.

She smiled, then stepped off the buggy and ran over to kiss him. "You are his favorite one."

"I like him."

"I like you, hombre." She shook her head. "It took you forever to get those pokey cattle up here."

"You can't run them to death."

With her shoulder, she wormed her way under his arm and drove a boob into his side as she hugged him. "You know how long you've been gone?"

"Too long." He waved Sobell over. "Put my horse up for me. I've got things to see about."

His partner rode over and took off his hat for her. "How are you doing, Silvia?"

"Fine. I'm glad he's back." Her face beamed as she swung on his arm.

Slocum handed him the reins to the gray. "Thanks, I'm going to call it a day. Think you can get them to Kansas?"

"Hey, they look stout to me. I hope the others that they're bringing in to go with them are that good."

Slocum helped Silvia onto the buggy. "I'll come out and look things over."

"They'll be here Friday, they told me."

"I'll be back here and help get them road branded," Slocum said, settling onto the seat and taking up the reins to Silvia's buggy horse.

"You two don't get into any trouble," Sobell said with a knowing grin and waved them on. "I like your new horses, hombre," he shouted as Slocum turned the buggy around and headed out.

Slocum waved that he'd heard him and winked at Silvia beside him. "He knows good horses too."

Possessively, she hugged his arm tighter as they headed for San Antonio. They ate supper at a nice restaurant, then took the rig to the livery and had the swamper care for the horse. Then, to the strum of guitars, they came up the street listening to the dancers' music and some girl singing a Mexican folk song. Silvia made him stop and hugged him.

"This is romantic," she said. With her head leaning on his chest and his arms holding her, they stood back in the shadows. The swivel of the dancers, like willows in a soft wind, made him glad to be there.

"Let's go to our room. I am jealous and think maybe some of these pretty girls would steal you away from me."

He laughed. "Not tonight."

"Oh, you never know."

Once in the hotel room, raw passion swept them away, and he forgot the cold nights sleeping on the ground alone without her smooth skin against his own, and she shared her muscular body, which carried him to new heights of pure fire. The scent of her filled his senses, and the entire process erased all the rest of his thoughts. Sleep became a peaceful suspension of time and he awoke early. Realizing her warm body was curled into him, he eased his way out from under the covers, leaving her to sleep, and dressed in the shadowy room.

He went to the restaurant and sipped on strong coffee on the patio as the small birds awoke. The night clerk brought him a letter. It had come from Cheyenne, from Crane's saddle shop, and contained a note from Wilma.

> *You said I could write you if I ever needed you. I don't need you right now.*
>
> *Houston and I plan to marry in May. Jennifer's husband came by Ten Sleep and cried with me last fall about her death. He wanted me to thank you. I lied and said I had no forwarding address. Two men were up here asking about you this winter. I told them nothing.*
>
> *One was Thomas Key and the other Hyde Walton. They were hired guns. Key has an eye patch, the other one wears glasses. Be careful. I will always think of you and our adventures.*
>
> *Love, Wilma*

More people wanting his hide. There would always be someone who might drop his name, or a drunk in a bar would mumble, "I know him. He was down at San Antonio this past winter."

It was early in the year to be having to head out from his winter nest, but he needed to leave no tracks. No place was sacred enough to hide from bounty hunters. He had enough of his share of the reward money left to be comfortable. His kitten upstairs in the bed would miss him, but she was fickle enough to find another before midnight. Sobell could bank Slocum's money in Kansas. He'd open an account up there at the Kansas railhead with instructions to pay Silvia's father his part. He closed his eyes. In two days he would be moving again.

He penciled a note to Wilma, thanking her for the warning and congratulating her on her future matrimony. Sent it to Mrs. Wilma Houston, General Delivery, Ten Sleep, Wyoming Territory.

He laid his plans to ride away. When he gave the news of his leaving to his spoiled hacienda owner's daughter, her response was as he expected—near hysterics. But she too would be all right. She loved San Antonio and the bright lights of a bigger place much more than the border town where he'd found her. With her looks and skills, she wouldn't sleep alone for very many nights.

On the third day, he rode the gray horse north in the darkness before dawn. He wore two shirts and his jumper, but the cold wind tried to chase him back to the Alamo Plaza. Instead, he kept riding on. He spent a few days in Fort Worth in the stockyard district, hoping the weather would warm, but March was not a promise keeper that winter was over.

Twice in Fort Worth, he saw Butch Cassidy and the Sundance Kid, dressed in tailored clothing and bowler hats. Once in a card game in the White Elephant Saloon's smoky atmosphere and the other time on a street corner with two well-dressed ladies of society in tow. They never acted like they recognized him.

He left Cowtown and stayed with an old friend near Denison. Hugh Barton and he had been together for a while right after the war. Barton found a sweet woman named Lisa and they had a passel of kids, and he farmed up there. They always made him welcome. The two adults with their five small children were cheerful company and the potbellied stove warm enough for him to linger a few days.

Slocum left thirty dollars in the Bartons' sugar bowl and rode on. It would be a long time till the cotton and corn harvest. The Indian Territory began north of the Red River Ferry. He went past the sign on the north bank that prohibited any alcohol being brought into the Indian Territory, with a stern warning that violators would be prosecuted to the fullest extent of the law by Judge Isaac Parker's Federal Court in Fort Smith, Arkansas.

The loss of a few days never bothered him, winding his way through the rolling hills going north. In the midst of an afternoon thunderstorm, he met an Indian woman. She was close to his age and straight-backed with premature gray streaking her long hair, which only added to her distinction and beauty. Even with a trade blanket for a shawl, there was nothing downcast about her. Mary Rose, she told him was her name, though she mostly went by just Rose.

They met casually when he took shelter from the downpour at a crossroads store's barn where they put up travelers. Rain had driven him and the gray horse he'd named Ghost to the shelter. She was already there when he dismounted at the doorway and led Ghost inside.

"Is this the place we can stay?" he asked the straight-backed woman standing in the shadows.

"Yes, this is his hotel." She about laughed at her own words. Amused anyway, and her smile looked inviting.

"Beats that rain out there." He turned an ear to more thunder in the distance. The patter of heavy drops on the cedar shingles came in waves overhead. He took his clammy slicker off, hung it on the saddle horn, and stopped to converse with this handsome woman.

"You have your family here?" He looked around.

"No, my family died last fall. Diphtheria took them."

"How sad you must be. Sorry I asked. Are you traveling alone?"

"Yes, there is a stomp. I decided I needed to go there."

"Good idea."

"Are you on a purpose?"

"Purpose?" He undid the cinch on the far side of his horse, straightened, and shook his head at her. "Nothing is pressing me."

"Maybe you would like to go to the event?"

"Would a white man be welcome?"

She shook her head, amused. "Sure. We aren't cannibals."

He chuckled and swung the saddle off his horse. "Good. I'll think about it."

The saddle on a rack, he led Ghost to one of the empty stalls. There was hay for him, and the pen looked secure. Slocum slid the bars in place and went back to Rose and the saddle. Undoing the bedroll, he asked her if she'd eaten anything.

"I'm fine."

"Well, would you eat some jerky?" He looked at her for a reply. "It's super good if you're hungry."

"I would chew on some," she said and stepped over to accept a bit of it he took out of a cloth bag.

He looked around. "Guess we can't make coffee in here."

She shook her head. "There are bunks in the back."

"Good." He shouldered his bedroll. "Lead the way."

There was a room he figured had once been a tack room. She pointed to a lantern and he dropped the bedroll, chewing on the peppery jerky. He lit a match and struck the wick. With the globe lowered, the lamp began to shed some light, and he hung it on the hook from the ceiling.

She nodded her approval. He sat down on the bench a small distance from her. "Where is the stomp being held?"

"On Sheephead Creek at a schoolhouse."

He didn't know the location. "Is that far away?"

"No. Maybe a four-hour ride."

"It starts tomorrow?"

"Tomorrow night."

He nodded that he heard her. "You're sure I won't get scalped?"

"Yes. No one will bother you. You will be my guest."

"I'd like to see it."

"Good, we can go up there in the morning."

"This rain passes, it will be cold again." He figured by dawn it would be down in the forties.

She agreed. "I am ready to sleep."

"Sure." He rolled out his bedroll on the floor, staying away from a few drips from above. She used one of the rough-made mattressless bunks to make her bed, and he blew out the lamp.

The storm grew greater in the night and woke him twice. Satisfied the barn was secure, he went back to sleep. They both woke in the predawn.

"There will be coffee up at the store," she told him, straightening her long skirt and blouse. Then she folded up her blankets.

"Good, I'm buying."

"I wasn't looking for an invitation."

"You invited me to the stomp."

"All right, I accept."

He saddled Ghost, tied on his bedroll, then helped her saddle her calico horse. The tricolor mare was tall for an Indian horse and it suited her, he decided. With his hands clasped for a stirrup, she stepped in and he tossed her into the saddle. Seated quickly, she thanked him. He swung onto Ghost, and they rode toward the store. Dismounting, they went inside, and the storekeeper's Indian wife greeted them. She had coffee and oatmeal for sale for twenty cents. He ordered two of each, after getting a head nod from Rose.

They ate their cereal near the warm woodstove, and the woman brought them coffee refills. She spoke to Rose about her going to the stomp. They conversed in English so Slocum understood most of the conversation. Obviously the store-keeper's wife wanted to attend but there was no way.

After the meal, they headed northwest on the narrow wagon tracks that wandered over some post oak–clad hills, and if they met someone coming back, they got off the road for them. By noon, they were at the schoolhouse grounds, and many families were camped all around the large meadow and even up in the woods.

"I know a woman who will sell us some food." Rose directed him and led the way through the camps. He felt several dark eyes following him, but nothing more hostile than gazes. The sun finally had warmed enough that they'd both stopped using blankets to keep warm.

"My sister, Renny," she said of the woman who came out of a sun-faded tent. The smile on the woman's face was one of welcome to both of them.

"I want you to meet Slocum," Rose said, dismounting. "He comes to see a stomp."

Renny shook his hand. She was perhaps a little taken aback by this white man accompanying her sister, but she recovered, offering them stew for lunch.

"We will eat with you," Rose said and waved for him to join her.

"Where do you live?" Renny asked, dipping out her rich-looking soup into bowls for them.

"I guess wherever I wear my hat." He thanked her for the steaming bowl and spoon.

Rose turned and smiled. "He's a cattle trader."

"Oh," Renny said. "Do you have a herd going to Kansas?"

"Yes, but a friend is taking it up there for me this year."

Renny looked impressed with him, and he could see she wanted to learn more about him and what he was to her sister, but didn't dare ask. Rose saved her. "He is just a friend who I met on the road."

Renny dismissed the matter and asked Rose about her farm. Rose told her that the she had some good sharecroppers on her place. Slocum had not thought about the widow being a large landowner, but obviously she owned some good bottomland.

The stew was delicious and, seated on a log, they both bragged on Renny's cooking. She poured them coffee and many people stopped by to talk to Rose. When Renny went off to get something, Slocum asked Rose privately if he should pay her for lunch.

With a smile, she dismissed the problem. No. Their horses hobbled, she took him around to meet more of her friends and relatives in the camp. There were sweets and treats and lots to eat. Some of the men talked to Slocum about their concerns. One older man said that Judge Parker would send his deputies there to arrest the whiskey traders—that he should be careful. Slocum promised him that he would be.

Rose took a towel and soap, then invited him to go take a bath with her. He agreed and in the warming sun, she led him to a more isolated place on the stream. By themselves, she looked at him, amused. "You have seen people naked. So you won't be shocked, will you?"

"No, I won't."

"Then let's bathe."

They undressed and waded into the cold water. "It won't take long to get washed," she said with a laugh. After soaping herself, she tossed him the bar of soap, rinsed, and hurried to get out. He admired her figure and then got busy lathering up. Soon he finished and waded out. Wet and cold, he stood shaking in the warm sun. She only had on her skirt, but coming to his aid, she stepped over to dry him.

"Was it cold enough?" she asked, busy drying him, and he caught her face and kissed her. Her firm breasts pressed against him, and she dropped the towel and put her arms around his neck.

When they parted, she wouldn't look at him. "I didn't bring you up here to seduce you."

"I guess we're both doing something we want to have happen."

A look of dismay swept her face. She shook her head. "I wasn't going to let this happen."

"It doesn't have to."

"Ha," she said. "It will happen, won't it?"

"You decide. Someone is coming," he said, hearing the chatter of voices. They hurriedly dressed and picked up their things. Three giggling teenage girls hurried by them, going back toward camp. Rose frowned. "Maybe they spied on us. That is bad manners."

"All they got was an eyeful," he said and put his arm around her shoulder.

She reached up and squeezed the hand he'd draped over her. "I am glad you are a patient man. I worried that if I found one, he would go crazy."

"I am really not patient," he teased.

"No. You are very polite. And I appreciate that."

"Where will we eat supper? I hate to bum food from your sister."

"Don't worry, she would do that to me. Besides, she is fascinated about how I found you and got you to come with me."

They both laughed.

A drunk came by her sister's camp while they were eating supper. "Why is there a white man here?"

Renny jumped up and pointed for him to go away. "Why is an impolite drunk in my camp asking questions he has no right to ask?"

He blinked at her. "Well, damn, aren't you bossy."

But he obviously wanted no part of the sharp-speaking woman and went off, about to stumble on his face. They laughed at his bumbling ways.

"Don't mind him," Renny said, sitting down again with her tall quiet husband.

"He is drunk. His tongue is too loose," he said. "We are glad to have you and Rose here."

"You bet." Rose got up and went to get some more fried potatoes and onions they had cooked with some sliced cured ham on the side.

"You want more?" she asked Slocum.

"No, I'm full. It was good."

At sundown, Rose led him toward the bonfire. She made a seat for them on a blanket and set another blanket close by in case it became cold during the night. Some friends came by and talked to her. She introduced Slocum to them. They were polite and then went on. He realized she was someone that many looked up to—her husband must have been a leader.

The drummers came and set up. Many wore traditional dress, and some had even painted their faces. Headdresses appeared, but none as spectacular as the ones the plains Indians wore. Most men wore eagle feathers attached to their unblocked hats. There were some women in deerskin-fringed dresses.

The dancing began slowly, and the special trains of men and women formed chains, and a chanter carried the rhythm of the song as they moved along at a very mesmerizing pace.

She leaned over to speak into his ear. "Are you watching them?"

He nodded.

"You think with your hands on my hips, we can do that?"

"I think so, if it doesn't get too fancy."

"Oh, we don't get too carried away." She pulled him to his feet. "This is social dancing, not war dances."

In a short while, they were stomping in a chain, and he imitated what she did. His hands on her hips, he followed and imagined what this willowy woman would be like in bed. She was a sweet person and acted like she didn't expect too much of him. His opportunity to make love to her would come later on. The sweet image of rapture under the blankets pushed him along as they shuffled to the chanter and the drums. The stomping was a contagious thing, and after a few trips she took him out of the line.

"You would make a good Choctaw," she whispered as they retrieved the blankets and went back to her sister's tent. "Could you and I sleep on one cot?"

"Would we sleep?" he asked her.

Amused, she shook her head. "Renny and her husband won't be back for hours. But we only have one cot."

"I'll be fine sleeping on the ground."

"No, you won't. Come on."

In the dark tent, they undressed, and she beat him under the covers. His gun placed close by, he kneeled on the cot edge to get under the covers, which she held up for him. His cool skin slid against her silky skin, and he knew the night would be wonderful even wedged on a single cot with her. In a dreamy world, they gently coupled like waves breaking on the seashore and sought each other's core. Exploring each other until they finally reached a high point, then swept onto a gentle plateau.

"I want you to stay and hold me."

"I'm not going anywhere tonight."

"Good." She kissed him, and they were back to working to get together again.

At dawn, he was up and dressed. He saw Renny under blankets on her side-by-side cot. She was holding her husband's fingers between them—both sound asleep.

Rose finished dressing and hurried to join Slocum. "I can make us coffee," she said. "You are leaving today?"

"There are things I must see about."

She nodded and went to work getting a fire going. "Saddle your horse. I will have it ready by then, I hope."

He bent over and kissed her. "Thanks."

With Ghost saddled and his bedroll tied on, he came back and squatted by her on the ground.

"When you ride back through here again, my place is on the Red River west of Nickmore in the bottoms. You can find me?"

"I can't say when, but if I get the chance, I will find you, Rose."

He ate her oatmeal sweetened with honey, which drew the saliva into his mouth. Sometimes it is better to ride off than linger, but he found Rose's company sincere and undemanding. Finished, he handed her the bowl, and they stood so he could hug and kiss her good-bye.

"Will you come by?" she asked.

"I can remember west of Nickmore. Thank you." He kissed her again and went for his horse. Magnets pulled at him, but it was time to go on. Leaving always was the hardest. But he rode on north that morning.

18

The latest cow town railhead was Newton, Kansas, right at Cottonwood Falls and about twenty miles north of the Arkansas River crossing. On the river there was a small place called Wichita where two whorehouses and that many saloons fed off the cattle herds going by and sold booze to the dry country across the river in the Indian Territory.

In Newton he found the banker he knew, Harvey Manning, in a tent with the fancy sign First Bank of Kansas. After explaining to Manning what he needed regarding the cattle money deposit and how to send Raúl his money, he visited a bar—also in a nearby tent—and had a beer. He was there way too early for any drovers to have arrived. The first cattle herds were still more than a month away, no doubt grazing down on the Trinity River and waiting for the grass to bust out.

After noticing all the temporary businesses, he asked Manning if there were plans for any permanent buildings to be built. The banker shook his head. "We won't be here that long. Newton hates cowboys and all their hell-raising so much that the city council is paying for half of the bond to move the railroad down to Wichita."

"Are you serious?"

"Two years is all I figure, and there won't be a railhead for loading cattle here."

Slocum frowned. "Man, folks got rich in Abilene."

"I know, but they won't listen."

He shook Manning's hand and thanked him. "I'm heading on."

There wasn't much wagon trade going west of York, Nebraska. The railroad was built clear to Cheyenne and headed west from there. But he followed the Platte River across Nebraska and looked at the desolate country wiped bare all along the old wagon route. No trees left, not even on the islands. All cut down for firewood. Places where the bluestems once grew head high were now dirt bare. Even many things like broken-down wagons had been salvaged until there weren't as many as when he was through there the last time. Lots of great grass plowed under and being homesteaded.

There was talk north of Ogallala that the government was going to buy out the Sioux and make it all homestead land to the South Dakota border. Word was they weren't using it anyway and white men would. He looked up his friend the sheriff in that town—once considered an outpost on the frontier and presently populated by more foreign-talking people than he ever knew. His sheriff friend complained about the horse thieves rustling every living animal they could. According to him, it was an obsession for them to steal any horse.

He thought about taking the train on to Cheyenne, but he'd much rather have the gray horse to ride when he got there. It wasn't late enough in the spring for the new grass—maybe three weeks short. So when his visit was over, he headed for Cheyenne on horseback.

The next town in western Nebraska was Lodgepole. He heard the whistle of a slow-moving freight train going east. He crossed the tracks and started up the main block of businesses. Things here looked less busy than they did in Ogallala. He stopped at a saloon, went inside, and bought a beer, then went and ate at the lunch counter. If you bought a beer in such a place, they set food out for their customers. Rich-tasting rye bread, cold cuts of roast beef and mustard, with a side of sauerkraut. Tasted much better than the jerky left in his saddlebags, and the beer washed it down.

"You going west?" the bartender asked, taking a break from polishing glasses.

"I'm headed for Cheyenne."

"Busy place? I've thought about looking for a job up there, but they treat me nice here. You a cattle man?"

"Yes, I have a herd coming up to the Kansas shipping yard."

"I thought you were one."

Slocum paid him for the beer and decided to ride on. Not much happening in the small town. He went out on the porch and watched two men come riding by. The man on the right wore an eye patch and his partner had on eyeglasses. He stepped back inside the batwing doors and signaled to the bartender to be quiet when he spoke to him.

"What's going on?" the man whispered, coming over, knowing something was wrong.

"Those two men getting off over at the bank. You know them?"

The man made a face watching them out the front window. "Never seen them before. Who are they?"

"I'm not sure, but when they pull their bandanas up, I'd say they were bank robbers."

"Holy shit!" He ran behind the bar for his shotgun.

Slocum saw the two pull up their bandanas, draw their guns, and go inside. "They're robbing the bank."

"You take the far side, I'll take this side of the street," the bartender said, holding the sawed-off scattergun beside his leg.

Slocum nodded and walked out of the saloon and directly for the saddle repair shop. A man came out the front door and greeted him.

Under his breath Slocum told him, "There are two masked men just went inside the bank."

A quick nod and the other man ducked inside the shop, then came out with a rifle. Slocum waved for him to stay close to the storefront. The door on the bank busted open, and the one with the eye patch came out and fired a shot in the air. His partner came behind him with two heavy sacks.

"Drop your guns," Slocum ordered and drew a bead on the money man. The man dropped both sacks and went for his gun. A blast of the bartender's shotgun and the one with the patch was knocked backward. Their horses, peppered no doubt by the shot, broke the hitch rail and trampled both of the two robbers, then tore out, dragging and stumbling over the rail until a bystander caught them.

A bald-headed banker in a suit rushed out the door. He and a clerk wearing a celluloid visor were frantically chasing greenbacks being blown around by the swirling wind. A man wearing a shining star on his long black coat came running with his gun drawn.

The two shot-up would-be bank robbers were on the ground, moaning over their wounds and the horse attack, when Slocum tossed their guns aside.

"What's going on here?" the out-of-breath lawman demanded.

"Them two went in and robbed the bank," the bartender said. "This man here saved the day, saw them and told me what they were up to, and we shot them coming out. He gave them warning what we'd do, told them to drop their guns. They wanted to fight."

"What's your name, mister?"

"John Slocum."

"Never met you," the lawman said. "You know these two outlaws?"

"Never seen them before in my life."

Bloody faced, the one wearing the eye patch looked hard at him. "You're the sumbitch I've been looking for."

"What for?" Slocum asked.

"To kill your ass."

"I haven't been in town fifteen minutes. Glad you missed me." His words drew some laughter from the bystanders.

Eye Patch ground his molars and shook his head in anger. Slocum smiled at the others. He for sure owed Wilma, or he'd never have noticed them coming into town.

"Mr. Slocum." The banker rose and dusted off the knees of his pants. "Let me shake your hand. My name's Simmons. You saved my bank and the depositors of this bank lots of money. I want to pay you a reward, sir."

Slocum wasn't going to turn down any reward. "These other two men need one too."

The banker agreed. "The three of you come back in an hour and I'll see all of you are rewarded."

The marshal sent for the doc to come and treat his prisoners. A crowd of the curious had been drawn by the activity. Talk of hanging them got the lawman's back up, and he silenced the ones talking about it.

"I can handle them," he said to the crowd. "Rufus, why don't you go set up a round for all of them over at the saloon," the lawman said to the bartender.

"I can handle that," Rufus said and broke open the shotgun, extracting the empty brass casings. "Everyone come with me. We're having a round on the marshal."

That drew most of the onlookers in a parade after the white-shirted man. Rufus nodded to Slocum to thank him and hurried back to his job. Things were settling down in Lodgepole. The doc arrived, looked over the two bloody robbers, and told the marshal to take them to the jail. He'd patch them up there. Several men hoisted the two up, and the lawman shook Slocum's hand.

"I don't know why that SOB wanted to kill you, but I can tell you one thing, I'm damn glad to meet you."

Slocum never told him anything about the reason those two were after him, shook the marshal's hand again, and then shook the saddle maker's too. "I'll hang around for a while and see what Simmons is going to do."

"I didn't do nothing," the saddle maker, Anderson, said.

"You were part of the force that stopped them. You'll get an equal part of it."

The mess was cleaned up. Their horses were sent to the livery, and luckily none of the shot did much damage to them. Slocum went back over to the saloon and had another beer. The crowd poked lots of questions at him, but he could only answer a few. He'd never laid eyes on those two. Had no idea why they were looking for him.

The clerk came over from the bank and reported that they had recovered all the money, and asked Rufus and Slocum to come over to the bank. Mr. Simmons wanted to pay them their reward.

"Get Anderson too," Slocum said to the man, and Rufus's boss told him to go too.

The banker met them on the boardwalk in front of his bank. The crowd gathered to hear him. "I appreciate these three men so much for saving the bank this morning. True heroes."

The applause was loud.

"I am giving a hundred dollar reward to each of them."

Slocum and his two cohorts nodded to one another. Slocum thanked Simmons and stuck the gold coins into his vest pocket. After another round of handshakes, Slocum thanked all of them, mounted Ghost, and rode on west.

The five twenty-dollar gold pieces jingled in his pocket, and a smile crossed his mouth. One more time he gave thanks to Wilma. He made it to Cheyenne three days later.

He put Ghost up at the livery, walked two blocks to the King's Arms Hotel, and signed in the registry. In the room at last, he dropped his bedroll and the saddlebags on the chair. Maybe a short nap would revive him. He'd been pushing himself hard since leaving Lodgepole. He needed a bath and a shave, but that could wait.

On his back looking at the square copper ceiling tile, he wondered if Carley had ever left an address for him at the saddlery. He got up, strapped on his six-gun, and put on his hat, then walked the four blocks. Inside the business, he discovered that Crane was busy waiting on a customer, and when the farmer left with his repaired harness on his shoulder, he nodded at Slocum.

"You looking for someone here?" Crane asked. The wide grin told Slocum she'd already been here.

"She lives north of town on Steele Hill. You can't miss her place."

"That the big white house up there?"

"You know it, then?"

"I've never been there, but I've seen the house. Thanks, I owe you one."

Gary shook his head. "You get the letter I forwarded?"

"Yes, thanks for that." He tossed him a twenty-dollar gold piece. "I owe you that."

"No, you—don't."

"Sometime when I have more time, I'll tell you all about it."

"I can't wait to hear. You ain't driving cattle to Kansas this summer?"

"I took a break. I better go see the lady. Thanks."

"I would too. She's some woman."

Slocum went and took a bath, got a haircut, and had a shave. The Chinaman laundered and ironed his clothes. It was near sundown when he rode up the driveway of the white house on Steele Hill. He turned to look back at the bloodred town in the evening light spread over the rolling hills turning green.

He hitched the horse and looked up at Carley's gasp when the door opened.

"Slocum, you did come back!" She flew into his arms, and they kissed.

"How have you been, Carley?"

"Oh, fine now that you're here. Let's put that horse up. You will stay a little while won't you?"

"Yes, I planned to if—"

She made a face and drove a fist into his belly. "You better. I have so much to tell you."

"Let's put Ghost up, then, since you halfway want me to stay."

"You tease. Bet you wonder how I landed all this place."

"Looks impressive," he agreed.

"Since you brought me here, I inherited my husband's family estate. He never told me much about them, except he came out West to prove that he could be successful. Lands, with his family's wealth he could have stayed home."

They both laughed.

With Ghost in the horse stall, she told the small man who worked for her to take good care of the gray. He nodded and shook Slocum's hand.

They went back to the house, and he quickly lifted her up in his arms and carried her through the front doorway. Her face looked so flushed with excitement that he worried this whole episode might be too much for her.

"Are you hungry or hungry?" she asked when he set her down.

"I can eat later."

"Good." Holding him by the sleeve, she took him upstairs.

Slocum spent most of the summer with Carley. She had planned to take a trip in August to see a cousin she'd found who lived in Omaha. Slocum wanted her to take the trip and knew his long spell in Wyoming might again bring killers on his trail.

He had Ghost re-shod and rode him enough to get him in shape. The day Carley was to leave for Nebraska, Slocum took her to the train, kissed her good-bye, and saw that the porter had all her luggage on board. She waved from the window under her wide-brimmed new hat, and he returned it.

He went and unhitched Ghost from the buggy that Wilburn, her man, had brought them into town in.

"I'll miss you," the old man said. "But I told my wife when you came that you weren't the marrying kind."

"Drive easy," he said, then mounted up and rode away.

Six weeks later, he was riding south in the Indian Territory. He spotted the sign for Nickmore, and it pointed west. He turned the gray and rode that way. It was getting dark when he stopped at the store and asked where Rose lived.

The man went outside and pointed down the road that went west. "You can't miss it. A big house on the right."

The man, who appeared to be a full-blood Indian, looked him hard in the eye. "Your name Slocum?"

"Yes. Why?"

"A medicine man told her a week ago you were coming. She's a grand lady and a good friend of mine. Tell her John Horseback talked to you."

Ghost must have felt his excitement; he single-footed the half mile. The calico mare whinnied at him in the pasture when she saw him. There was the big house, and he rode up the lane.

Rose was standing on the porch with her arms folded— waiting.

"Where have you been, big man? You were supposed to have been here two days ago."

Two days ago? He had no idea what she meant. When he dismounted, a boy came to take his horse and very politely said, "I'm glad you made it."

"Thanks," he said to the youth.

He shook his head and went to hug her. "How have you been?" he asked. "Who told you I was coming?"

"A real medicine man. Never mind. You are here now."

"John Horseback said to be nice to me."

With a grim head shake, she squeezed him and then laughed. "I don't believe that either."

"Well, he said something like that anyway." He took her arm and they went to the front steps. He looked up at the two-story house with columns and nodded. "Nice place."

"Better than an old barn, huh?"

"No, those were sweet times. I'd never have stopped except for the rain and you showing me how to stomp."

"That wasn't much."

"Hey, I loved every minute of that night."

She opened the door and winked at him. "A one-cot deal and—"

"Hey, that was neat too. You told me if I ever came this way to come by and see you."

She looked up the staircase and then at the finely furnished living room. "Oh, hell with it. Let's go upstairs." She lowered her voice. "And do it."

They flew up the hardwood stairs and she guided him into a bedroom with a tall poster bed and a gentle wind moving the lace curtains in the open windows.

Slocum toed off his boots, and Rose asked him to undo the lacing on the back of her dress. With his eyes shut, he fumbled to undo her dress and recalled their night in a narrow cot. Drums rumbled in his ears, and he could hear the chanter. Damn, this would sure be fun.

Slocum spent the fall with her, attending several stomps, and the two of them grew even closer. She read a story to him in the *Fort Smith Elevator* newspaper, how two killers were hung in Cheyenne. When she finished, she dropped the paper and looked at him. "Isn't that the two you chased into Yellowstone?"

"Yes, and it is good day that those two won't ever kill or hurt anyone again."

When the frost turned the oak leaves red and gold, he saddled Ghost one morning and rode on. It was time for him to frequent the plaza in San Antonio. He waved at his friend standing on the porch with her arms folded and shaking her head. Maybe the medicine man would know when he would be back—he jabbed Ghost with a spur and he responded in a short lope. They were headed for the Alamo.

Watch for

SLOCUM ON THE SCAVENGER TRAIL

396th novel in the exciting SLOCUM series
from Jove

Coming in February!